A Slice of Carmel

A Jaden Steele Mystery

Barbara Chamberlain

Barbara Chamberlain

Cups of Gold Publishing | Los Gatos, California

For Dr. Tanya Johnson

The editor and inspiration for this story

The sea has been a magnet for the curious from the beginning of time.

When Jaden Steele saw Monterey Bay, she felt a kinship with the restless waves. The young widow decided to move and start a new life near the rolling surf of the Pacific Ocean. Every furious crash of breakers on the brown jagged rocks called to her like sirens of legend lured ships to the deep.

Next time you go to the sea, watch the waves and you will feel the same way.

Barbara Chamberlain

August. He kept his swollen eyes open only enough to see the pretty woman from the store. She ran down the alley to the door of the downstairs parking garage, pausing for a moment to lift something shiny out of her jacket. He caught the glint of a knife blade. She shook her head and dropped the knife back into her pocket. The woman might have noticed him. Maybe not, because of the dark night. He pressed his back against the wall between two big fuchsia bushes. Tonight he had seen three other people in the alley. Usually there might be one, maybe two.

He remembered that she was kind. *Pretty with dark curly hair and sparkling dark blue eyes.* Gone were the fog and the blankness that made him forget so much of the time. He remembered the knife lady's kindness in letting him eat food from the table in the court. The good meal helped him feel better, made him think without the fog in his mind. There was a buried memory somewhere in the mist that he could never snatch back.

A scream from the downstairs parking garage split the cold, foggy night air.

He jumped up. *They would blame him!* Gasping, he ran to the street, dashing the six blocks down to the safety of the dark beach.

I should have gone to help her. She was a nice lady. What's the matter with me? I didn't help that other lady either. Still gasping and wheezing, he finally reached the beach. He dove into the familiar white sand and heaved up all the good food.

The shadowy memory of better times vanished like the ocean in a fog.

His world spun like he was on a merry-go-round except the horses looked like sharp fanged gargoyles who snapped at him.

Previous April. Jaden Steele swept up her seminar notes and tossed them into her black leather briefcase as her students left the Surf and Sand meeting room at Asilomar conference center. She felt a shadow next to her before she glanced up to see a brilliant smile on the handsome, olive-skinned face. Sergio Martelii, his name tag read. He must have asked five questions during the morning lecture. Jaden decided that he was the one person in the class who did not need to attend a communication seminar. She remembered that Sergio had introduced himself as the representative from a local city council. He planned to return and train his fellow Carmel city council members.

"Have you been over to Asilomar Beach yet?" he asked, his dark eyes focused on her.

"No, I came into the Monterey airport last night. By the time the shuttle van brought us here it was dark and foggy. I was exhausted and went straight to bed. This morning, though, I woke up to the most compelling view of the Pacific, the brilliant white sand, and the waves crashing on those dark rocks. It's one of the most spectacular ocean views that I've ever seen. With that scenery I could barely concentrate on the class."

"Paradise," Sergio's dark eyes sparkled. "You are from Nebraska, aren't you? From here we can walk to the beach on the boardwalk over the sand from just below this meeting room. I'd be happy to show you. You haven't been here before, or seen the Seventeen-Mile Drive or the Carmel Mission? You must visit them."

Why not? Jaden thought, enchanted by the change from the view of cornfields from her lonely house in Kearney, Nebraska. Even though she enjoyed teaching, something inside of her was desperately seeking an elusive fugitive ghost that would make her feel less like a caterpillar and more like a butterfly. She needed wings.

"That sounds very nice. Let me change my clothes and I'll meet you at the beginning of the boardwalk in about twenty minutes."

Half an hour later, Sergio walked beside her on the gray boardwalk over the sand until they reached the two lane road that followed the beach to a point of restless waves. When the road was safe to cross, they walked to the water's edge. He was only an inch or two taller than her five feet seven inches, but how handsome with that dark, wavy hair and those deep brown, almost black, eyes. He worked at keeping those muscular arms and flat stomach. Jaden guessed that he must be at least ten years older than her own thirty-four years. He was wearing a navy blue bathing suit that showed the dark hair on his muscular chest

She, safely she thought, wore her antique powder blue sweats.

Jaden knew her favorite sweats brought out the clear dark blue-violet of her eyes. Besides the black suit she wore at the seminar, her only other outfit was the slacks and light sweater she wore on the plane from Nebraska. After two years of flying to these seminars, she found traveling with one carry-on saved a lot of trouble and expense.

The brilliant white sand, beaten for eons by huge breaking waves, stretched as far as she could see to both points. More seagulls than she could count circled in the clear blue sky above them. From their easy, circling glides, the sea birds eyed that shifting line where the sand met the tips of the waves. Pelicans stood on the jagged rocks, not the least bit frightened of the swirling water.

"What is that complex on the hill?" Jaden asked about some white buildings on the hillside.

"The Inn at Spanish Bay," Sergio answered with a smile. "I have my car and can take you on a tour of the Seventeen-Mile Drive. The other direction is beautiful, too. Beyond that point are downtown Pacific Grove and Lover's Point."

"In Nebraska, it's flat everywhere. The view is magnificent. I've never been anywhere like this. The sand is so white." She breathed deeply of the moist salt spray. "Let's sit down and watch the ocean. I wish I could take this scene home."

They flopped down on the soft sand. The breeze off the ocean blew Jaden's dark curls in front of her eyes. The dark hair was a gift of those Roma gypsy descendents who had been her paternal great-grandparents. While waves of settlers took wagon trains west, her family stopped the gypsy roaming forever in Kearny, Nebraska. Grandfather became a butcher, and married an orphaned Yorkshire woman. And they were married fifty-five years before she died. An expert in knives, he made his own and also sold them. Unless it was a rifle, nothing was more prized than her grandfather's knives. If only she owned more than one now. Even though Grandpa had been dead for twelve years, she still missed him. The pleasant memories of Grandpa Abel Cooper and Grandma Ethel always brought a smile to her face.

"You have a beautiful smile," Sergio commented, taking her hand in his.

Jaden could not help thinking how much he reminded her of her husband, Brent, when he took her hand, rubbed it against his face, then kissed it.

Her mind whisked back to the time she and Brent had spent together. Their blissful marriage of only five years had been shattered by one visit from two policewomen. Brent died instantly when a drunk driver swerved over to hit his car head on. She carried the pain that he had not suffered. Whenever she thought of him, her eyes burned with tears.

Even now, to fight the tears, Jaden closed her eyes tightly to blot out her memories. *Everyone leaves me,* she thought with a crashing wave of self pity. Sergio's gentle hand cupped her chin and turned her head slightly as his lips met hers. A deep longing seized her and she slipped her arms around his chest. The passion of his kiss made her forget Brent, the beach, the ocean, the shrieking cries of the seagulls.

Surprised by what she had just done, Jaden pulled back. She forced herself to say, "I'm sorry, Sergio. This is a little too fast for me." She fought down a wave of desire.

"Jaden, I understand." He traced the back of his fingers along her arm. She shivered and almost gave in to kissing him again. "Let me take you to dinner tonight and show you Monterey. You would like that. It's better than sitting alone in your room."

She looked at the wild ocean beating on the ancient granite rocks and felt a deep kinship with those waves. She wondered if he could sense her loneliness, or simply turned on his obvious charms for most females. Jaden suspected the latter, but quickly buried her thought.

"That sounds wonderful. Thank you."

"You're beautiful. I can tell that you love the sea as I do. Asilomar Beach is a perfect place to watch the waves. This is going to be the best week of my life! Tonight I'm going to take you over to Cannery Row in Monterey and out to dinner there or on the wharf."

She sighed deeply. "I'd love it." Jaden realized this was exactly what she needed.

This must be what her mind was seeking after five painful years of mourning for Brent. She found an exciting man in a beautiful area. *I want to stay here forever.* How could she leave her teaching position at the University of Nebraska?

Sergio took her on a whirlwind tour of Monterey that evening. She thought that this must be like being struck by lightning.

About midnight she told him, "Sergio, I have to teach a class in the morning."

"I'll take your class," he said. "What shall we do tomorrow afternoon?"

Monday he had breakfast with her in the dining hall at Asilomar. They picked up their trays and sat at a table by a picture window overlooking the Pacific. "I'm going back to work at the gallery after your class."

"There's emails from my students. Someone wants to turn in their mid-term assignment late. Someone can't do the assignment at all. If they only knew that I get the same emails from students every semester. There are messages from the chair of the communication department. No one seems to realize that this is spring break."

He put his hand on her arm and spoke gently, "Tonight you will forget about everything. We will have dinner at one of my favorite restaurants on Highway 68 by the airport. The food is excellent and there is a good variety."

On the day for her to fly home they exchanged addresses. She slipped his business card into her oversized black leather purse.

"When I get a chance, I'm coming to see you," he promised. "There must be artists in Nebraska who want to sell their paintings."

Sergio was a partner in a Carmel art gallery and a member of the City Council.

She had wanted to visit his gallery, but they had been too busy seeing the sights in Monterey. Jaden promised herself that someday she would visit his gallery and do more than just drive through the city of Carmel-by-the-Sea. She forced herself to fly back to her empty home and to read another batch of papers on the history of communication. There must be some teaching positions in the California universities.

Sergio called her at least once a week.

When she longed to hear his voice, she called the gallery. A Vincent Howard, who introduced himself as Sergio's partner, always put her directly through to him.

At night she relived that precious moment on the sand when he kissed her or when he kissed her the last time in the Monterey airport lounge.

Jaden began to dread going home to her empty house and her frustration, especially on the long weekends. One night her doorbell rang. Through the viewer she saw Sergio.

It was like a dream. "Sergio! What are you doing here in Kearny?"

He embraced her. "Purchasing paintings. You have artists here. I wanted to surprise you." He stepped in. She responded to him with the passion of years of loneliness.

He stayed for the weekend. "I must go. I will be back when I can."

Jaden spent a lonely month longing for Sergio and the beautiful white sand that bordered the haunting, restless Pacific, when she found a treasure on the internet. She was looking at California university employment sites, then jobs and businesses when she saw an ad:

Cutlery business for sale in Carmel.

Before she called the owner, Jaden went to the bottom desk drawer and pulled out her grandfather's knife and dark brown leather sheath, the one he always wore. Local legend said grandfather could cut off a man's fingers before the man could pull the trigger of a gun.

Jaden had never seen any loose fingers in the shop. At the grinding wheel one day, she asked her grandfather, Abel, about the story the children at school had told her.

"Keeps people from bothering us, don't it, Jaden? Hey, you're learning to grind really well." His huge, scarred thumb rubbed the sharp edge. "You'll be making your own knives in no time." He made knives and sold them in the butcher shop. *Beautifully crafted knives. Hand polished bone handles*. People might manage without a gun, but a knife had more uses than Jaden could count. Though the knives made their family prosperous, Grandpa would never believe the prices they commanded today.

Against Grandmother's protests Grandpa Abel had taught Jaden how to throw knives. When the gypsies performed anywhere in Europe, he claimed his father was the star of the show. With a lump in her throat Jaden stared at Grandpa Abel's knife. *I was only six or seven years old when my gramps started me polishing, grinding, and throwing knives.* The name A. Boxt jumped out at her from the top of the bone handle. A for Abel and Boxt, simply a gypsy or possibly her family's word for knife. If only she had more of them now. Yesterday she found one for sale again on eBay for $1650. The prices were inflating rapidly.

It was unlike her to be so adventurous. Jaden knew her decision had been made. After negotiations with the owner, and checking and double-checking all the business details, she and her attorney finalized the contract. "The terms are great," he told her. "You even have first option to buy the Dolores Court property."

"That would be a miracle." Jaden toured and re-toured the shop on a virtual reality internet site made available to serious buyers. She studied the inventory list and the financial records. The seller, Hal Lamont, did not have the biggest expense, the lease, because he owned the property.

"The business is in a court on Dolores Street," the owner explained. "Above the four businesses are six two bedroom apartments. If you want mine, and will manage the property, you can have your place rent free."

I'll do it. Jaden could not wait to leave her treading water existence for a new life. She did not want to spend the rest of her days living in the house her grandparents had left her. The ghosts of Grandma and Grandpa and Brent drifted through every room as eternal shadows. She felt like the people in the old wagon trains that stopped to supply in Kearny must have felt. There was a better world in the west. *The promised land.*

Wouldn't she surprise Sergio?

Early in July Jaden walked up to Dolores Street Court from Carmel Beach. She stared into the plate glass windows of her new store, "A Slice of Carmel." To enter the court, visitors walked by that window. *Great location.* Through the two windows, one on Dolores and the other on the court, she saw the outdoor tables that must belong to the tea shop. She walked into the welcoming stone patio, her heart thumping with excitement.

Impressionistic splashes of red fuchsias and yellow marigolds peered over the white window boxes of the second story court apartments. To the left of her shop was a gallery specializing in California art, and next to the cutlery store was a vacant shop that was probably a victim of the economy. The Mad Hatter's, a coffee house and small café took up the entire right side of the court. Five white outdoor tables and royal blue market umbrellas made the sand colored flagstone patio look so comfortable that Jaden reminded herself that she would have to run the store.

"Jaden!" Hal Lamont called from the door of her new business.

On the phone Hal had again promised, "If you want my apartment and will manage the property, it is yours. Mine's the corner one and has a great view of the park."

What a clincher. After checking the rents in the area, Jaden thought she might have to live in the shop. The sale of her home in Nebraska brought a small fraction of the funds she would need. With financial care, it would all work. She felt lucky that her agreement with him included his working with her daily for three months and then two days a week for the rest of the year.

Though Hal was helping her a lot by giving her his apartment, there was no question that she would have to be tightfisted. *Hal must be about seventy years old.* White hair framed his smooth face. *One of those men who become more handsome with age.*

His smile, quick and easy, made him the perfect type of person to deal with the public.

"Where did you park?"

"I found a spot on Junipero where there is all day parking five blocks from here. Walked down to the beach first, though."

"I'm sorry I forgot to tell you that we have a parking garage and laundry room underneath the court. The entrance is on Fifth. You'll need your own remote to drive in there anyway."

Jaden breathed a sigh of relief. A parking space here was almost better than an apartment. Most of the spaces were ninety minutes, too short an amount of time for people to stroll the shops and eat, let alone work all day. Jaden surveyed the familiar cases filled with an amazing inventory that she had seen in the computer virtual reality tour of A Slice of Carmel.

Hal pointed out his exclusive ceramic line of knives. "It's a great seller. Ceramics like Gideon rarely need sharpening. They've come out with a black blade that's even better."

Hal carried a large variety of chef's knives, his best sellers. They also, of course, provided a sharpening service. Next to galleries, Carmel was full of restaurants and chefs who wanted and needed sharp blades.

The new owner noted William Henry knives and the Detloffs, admiring aloud about the outstanding craftsmanship.

"You know something about cutlery." Hal sounded surprised. "Please don't be offended, but I never expected a woman to buy the business."

"I was raised by my grandparents after my parents died in a flu outbreak," she explained. "My grandfather, Abel Cooper, was a butcher who also made knives. You never forget those childhood experiences."

"Abel Cooper was your grandfather?" Hal's gray eyes widened. "Do you have any of his knives? They are so unique."

"Just one, unfortunately," she answered, thinking about how she sold her home, the one her grandparents left her, to buy into the store.

Customers were strolling in and out of the shop. She admired how Hal took out a knife when a customer asked, and placed it on a black velvet square. He began a subdued sales pitch. "This blade rarely needs sharpening."

She learned quickly that if a customer reached over to pick up and hold the knife, a sale was likely.

Jaden walked over to a wall case that contained about twenty swords from ancient to modern. The price tags made her blink.

"Do you sell these, Hal?"

"Every once in a while," he answered. "Only one last year. They are great conversation pieces, though. They're visible through the glass storefront, so tourists walk in just to see them. This is summer, but weekends and holidays there are always lookers. Don't ever be surprised if some of these wanderers turn out to be buyers."

"Everything is in cases," she commented. "At least that makes them safer."

"When they ask to see something, bring out this black velvet pad." A quick smile sprang to his lips. "Borrowed the idea from a jewelry store. I never bring out more than two. If they want to see something else, put one back in the case. This inventory is too expensive to lose. Might as well discourage thieves as much as possible."

Jaden nodded. Under his expert sales guidance, she learned all morning.

"They go to you first thing, have you noticed?" Hal commented, his clear gray eyes sparkling. "Can't blame them for that. Are you hungry? Let's go out for tea or coffee and a great Mad Hatter's sandwich."

He adjusted the hands of a paper clock below a closed sign to half an hour from now, and locked the door. "Everyone is used to this here. Most shops can't afford much help. Some are just a one person operation like this most of the time, so if you are gone, the shop is closed."

They sat at one of the outdoor tables. Jaden slipped on her sunglasses and picked up the menu. She gulped at the $2.50 price for a cup of tea or house coffee. Like Dorothy Gale, she was not in Kansas (or Nebraska) any more. A tall man wearing a light blue denim apron approached the table with a steaming mug of coffee that he sat in front of Hal. The waiter had sandy hair graying at the temples. His smile made Jaden feel at ease.

"Hello and welcome to Carmel!" He was wearing an apron with the Mad Hatter's hat on the center front and scenes from Alice in Wonderland printed all over it.

Jaden grinned up at him. "Thank you. So happy to meet you."

"My name is Kyle Foster. I'm one of the owners of this café. My dear, we have all been waiting to meet you! Hal has been talking nothing but retirement."

"He's going to train me first and then work for a year, so he is not quite retired."

"Since none of us thought he would ever retire, he's making progress. Now don't say a word of protest, you two, but this lunch is our treat. What would you like?"

"Thank you, Kyle. That is not necessary," Hal protested. "I was going to treat Jaden."

"Oh, yes it is. You can't say another word. Jaden, choose anything at all."

Jaden ordered a tuna and avocado croissant sandwich from the six sandwich choices. There were six different salads offered, too. Each one sounded better than the next. *Green salad with pine nuts and dried cranberries. Romaine with pineapple and strawberries. Spinach with pecans. Chinese chicken salad. Baja-Mixed greens with shredded Pepper Jack. Chef's Anything Surprise.* Her mouth watered.

"And I'll have iced tea."

"What variety do you like?" Kyle tapped the bottom of the menu.

Jaden saw twenty types of tea listed. "Bring me your favorite, Kyle."

He nodded and turned back toward the small restaurant entrance.

"Kyle and his partner, Sydney, run the business and also do wedding planning and catering for special events," Hal explained as he drank his coffee. "They're both chefs. The menu is simple and that makes it easier to manage. Their catering is superb. The best in the area."

"Carmel has so many galleries and places to eat. How do all these galleries stay in business, Hal? I counted six in the block coming here, and there is one in the court." Though she was tempted to ask him about Sergio, she kept quiet.

"Sometimes I wonder myself. People do come here to buy art," Hal answered. "Gene Miller at the California Gallery just gets by. The empty store was a gallery. The town is full of chefs, too. I'm sure that's why Kyle and Sydney opened their own business." He leaned closer to her to whisper, "Chefs buy a lot of knives, though, Jaden. I'm always thankful for that."

A busboy that Hal introduced as Enrique brought Jaden a tall glass of tea.

"This iced tea is wonderful." She squeezed the slice of lemon into the ice on top. "I think it is orange pekoe with just a little flavor of berries."

"They make the best coffee in town, too."

"Here you are." Kyle set their plates on the table. Slices of fresh pineapple and whole strawberries the size of plums garnished her plate. Her mouth watered.

"How is your tea?" he asked.

"Excellent." She guessed the blend correctly.

"But it's my own creation, *with* caffeine," he warned. "Some day a study will come out on the brighter side of caffeine. Sorry to leave you but we're getting busy. Enjoy lunch."

"Thank you," Jaden and Hal said together as Kyle moved to another table.

"This tuna did not come from a can," Jaden said after the first delicious bite.

"You don't have to go anywhere else in town for food or coffee, Jaden."

"Hal, I've been going over several ways to introduce myself to the community. How about a new ownership open house for the cutlery shop? Invite the whole town. What do you think? I could ask Kyle and Sydney to cater."

"It's a great idea! Everyone's been wondering about you anyway. The only thing about Kyle and Sydney is…." Furrows deepened in Hal's normally smooth forehead.

"What is it?"

"Oh, very little chance of some problem, but at the time of 9/11, Kyle and Sydney closed the shop, went to New York, and helped with food for workers during the search operations. They realized a need for something like that for emergencies, so they started a non-profit charity, designed and purchased a large van, and lined up volunteers willing to help. They're coordinated with the Salvation Army, the Red Cross, and a local Lions Club. If they are called, they will close the café and leave immediately. They did it during the wildfires in Santa Cruz."

"That's amazing!" Jaden said. "What a needed project. After some of our tornadoes, help like that was needed right away. Some people are left with nothing. You have some interesting tenants in Dolores Street Court."

"Yes. There's Bobbi Jones who lives next to you. She works at the library and has only been here five months. Very quiet lady. Carmel police sergeant, Bill Amirkhanian, Kyle and Sydney, Esther Stennis, who admits to being 86 and has more energy than most 40-year-olds, and…" his voice lowered, "Emile Von Otto."

"That's an odd name." Jaden sipped her tea.

"He's an odd person. The last time I saw him was when he rented the place two years ago. Emil Von Otto. I doubt it's his real name."

"You're kidding, but there could not be many Von Ottos in the whole world."

"I know he's there sometimes because of the garbage. I figure he keeps it for a vacation place. He doesn't seem to drive a vehicle. Whoever drops him off drives a silver Porsche. Pays the lease a year in advance. I figure he's better than some tenants who play the music too loud. For sure, no one complains about him."

Jaden sipped her refreshing iced tea, wondering about her odd assortment of neighbors.

She fumbled for the right word, "A unique group of people live in Dolores Court."

"You're right about that. I'm really ready to retire, Jaden. Do you think you could manage the apartments and the store, too?"

"I won't know until I try."

"In a few days we'll ask Kyle and Sydney about a party to introduce you to the city and the city to you. I've lived here forty years so the open house is a good idea. The party should satisfy everyone's curiosity." He raised his steaming coffee mug in a toast. "Good luck, Jaden."

After two weeks, once Jaden settled the small amount of personal items she had brought with her, she tried to call Sergio. "He's on a buying trip," his business partner, Vincent Howard, explained. "Should be back in about a week. Would you like to leave a message for him?"

"No. No. I'll call again. Thank you."

On her walking tours of the town, she walked by the Martelli and Howard gallery every day without seeing him. One day, intrigued by a large, breathtaking oil of the Monterey Bay area in the window of the gallery, she strolled in. Some of the artist's other works, all of the Monterey Bay area, hung on the back wall. The paintings were at least three by five feet. They reminded her of her dream-like meeting with Sergio. Jaden realized that her brief time with him did not mean love. She still felt annoyed and hurt at being ignored. By now she realized it must be deliberate.

The sudden voice at her side made Jaden start. "Aren't they magnificent?"

"Yes." She cleared her throat. "What a talent for capturing the beauty of this area."

"We agree. We are the exclusive dealers for his works." He handed her a card.

Vincent Howard, Art Sales. Martelli and Howard Gallery. He was probably three inches taller than Jaden. His light brown hair was thinning at his forehead.

"Thank you."

The man's hazel eyes narrowed. "Do I know you? Do you come here on vacations?"

Since Jaden knew his voice, he probably recognized hers. "No. I'm...I'm just looking. Thank you so much." She fled outside and walked rapidly through the tourists until she reached First Murphy Park on the corner of Lincoln and Sixth, diagonally across from the main library. Jaden sat down on the bench next to the sitting bronze statue of the old man and woman to catch her breath. Two other benches on the corner completed a U shape where people could rest, eat lunch, and watch the constant passing parade of eclectic tourists.

She envied the couple, "Valentine," perpetual in their serene pose.

If only Brent.... She fought back the tears that she knew were for herself.

Suddenly a soft foreign voice next to her made her jump. She turned to face a smiling young man.

"Excuse me," said a man with a possible German accent, "would you take our picture?"

Jaden looked at the man's companion, a dark-haired woman who was also smiling at her. "Oh, of course. Would you like to sit on either side of the Valentine statue?"

As Jaden looked into the preview picture of the camera, and said, "Smile," they smiled that smile of a couple in love. Her eyes misted over again. *What is the matter with me today?*

"Thank you, misses," said the young woman with her charming accent.

"You are very welcome," Jaden answered, "Enjoy your visit here."

"Yes. Thank you," the man answered. "First we are walking to the beach, and next going to Big Sur and Hearst Castle. Could you tell us where is the mission?"

Jaden gave the two directions thinking of her walk in the beautiful Carmel mission garden with Sergio. "This mission has been restored," Sergio had told her.

She did not want to be rude, but the young couple's happiness reminded her of her honeymoon and short life with Brent. He was not only a lover but her best friend. She met him, of all places, when she went to a self defense class that he taught. He was astonished when he learned how well she handled and threw knives. She told him about her grandfather and growing up helping him make knives. Losing Brent left a deep black gorge in her life that she knew she must bridge to make a future for herself. A shadow of uneasiness crept into her thoughts. This might not have been the way to change her life. *The bay is so beautiful, though.* She finally admitted to herself what she already suspected. Her rush to banish loneliness had made her suspend her common sense.

"I have to go back to work now," she explained to the young couple. "Have a nice visit." She rushed back to Dolores Street Court.

Entering the store, she literally bumped into Kyle. "My dear. Out jogging for your lunch? How far did you walk? Your face is flushed. You need some iced tea."

She was breathing hard, too, as though she had just finished a race. "Thanks, Kyle. I have ice water in the fridge."

Jaden took some deep breaths to calm herself as they entered the shop together.

"I've discussed your 'coming out' party with Sydney," Kyle told her. "He thinks it's a great idea. We love parties. We'd like your input."

"Do you have an approximate cost?" Jaden asked, wondering if the party was going to ruin her yearly profits.

Kyle smiled, "You are so delightfully Nebraska. I'll bet you shop at sales."

Jaden's face, which had been cooling down, flushed again. *Of course she did.*

"Sorry, my dear. I apologize. I'm so used to dealing with rich clients."

After his customer left, Hal walked over to join their conversation.

Outside, Jaden saw the young Enrique, who often worked as a busboy at the café, begin to clean their windows. She had wondered how they stayed so sparkling.

"Cut the philosophy," Hal asked, "What do you want for the open house treats?"

Kyle protested, "It's not philosophy, Hal. It's truth. Have you ever met anyone who came to this area to look for a bargain sale? Don't get me wrong, Jaden. I was raised in Kansas right in the middle of acres and acres of corn. Tons of normal people would ask prices and look for sales. I'm just trying to get Jaden to understand the customers here. Some never ask about price."

"You mean if you have to ask you can't afford it? That seems unreal to me. Kyle, how much do you want for the catering?" she asked.

"Well, Sydney and I love our one ceramic knife. We would like the rest of the set in trade for our catering services that afternoon."

The Gideon knives were actually man-made diamond blades, all of them black or white, hot pressed and fired simultaneously, and rarely needed sharpening. The process of manufacturing the newer black ones with a special additive made them even better. *Very expensive.* Kyle was asking a lot for the afternoon's catering.

She looked at Hal.

"It's your store," he commented.

"Done." Jaden shook his hand. "This is what they would do in Kearny. But we're also going to put it in writing if you two don't mind."

Both men laughed.

"Tonight, my lovely Jaden Steele, you will have dinner at our place. We can tell you some of our ideas for the party. You haven't met Sydney outside of the kitchen. We'll invite whoever of the neighbors can come! We have not had company for dinner in ages."

A bouquet of white iris and pink carnations transformed the dining table at Kyle and Sydney's into what looked like a picture in a magazine. The contrast between Jaden's apartment and theirs startled her. The white linen tablecloth, blue and white Wedgwood china, and rose patterned sterling silver utensils on the perfectly set table looked so inviting. A photographer for a home magazine should be here, she thought.

Hal, a widower, introduced her to his friend, Sandy, a lively sixty-five year old woman in a white pants suit with a sequined collar, who worked at the Carmel Foundation. She already knew the gray-haired woman who must be nearing forty, but looked older. Esther was there. "You've met Bobbi Jones? And Esther?"

"Yes," Jaden answered with a smile. She had tried inviting Bobbi for walks down to Carmel Beach. The librarian appeared so uncomfortable that she usually went home after about five minutes. Bobbi wore no make-up, thick glasses, and eternally a baggy, polished cotton black suit. Sandy and Bobbi made Jaden think of a princess and a pauper. Bobbi's skin was perfect, though. Jaden's mind jumped to how she could help her get into a little more stylish mode. A desire to dive in and do one of those total makeovers often overwhelmed Jaden. She could almost envision an attractive woman in Bobbi's place. First, the woman should never wear black. And why would she wear a suit that looked too large for her? Any thrift store had better clothes. What terrible taste. A little make-up would not hurt, either.

Jaden scolded herself. She was being catty. This was not like her. Something about the woman triggered a spark in her mind. *Forget it. You have enough to think about.*

Esther often joined her on a walk to the beach. Jaden found her amazing with a sharp mind that missed nothing. One time she mentioned her worry about Bobbi.

Esther answered, "Your worry about Bobbi is well-founded. She often leaves the beach after ten minutes. There's more to Bobbi Jones than we know. Her behavior is not natural."

She had to admire Esther's insight When Jaden left her to jog on the beach, Esther would wave good-bye, and turn to go by the market or walk up Scenic Drive to the mission. The older woman also volunteered four hours a week at Harrison Library.

She's got more energy than I do. I need more rest. The battle with the dark circles under my eyes is lost. I want to look sensational the next time Sergio sees me.

Everyone else in town seemed to know that she had bought the cutlery shop. Sergio had not contacted her in six weeks. Maybe he was on a buying trip. How long would one of those trips last? She wished she had another phone number besides the gallery. Sergio's silence was the one annoying problem during her first six weeks in the resort town. She had been so busy, though. For some reason the man usually lurked way in the back of her thoughts. Jaden began to wonder if she actually had wanted him or desperately wanted a change in her life because she had lost Brent and was lonely.

Kyle broke into her thoughts. "I'd like you to meet Bill Amirkhanian."

The man was almost as tall as Kyle's approximately 6'2" and was more muscular. He looked like he weight trained every day. Though he did not smile, his dark hair and dark eyes reminded her of Sergio's. His eyes were more penetrating, though. More serious.

Bad sign. Why are those memories popping up in the middle of this dinner party? She swallowed a lump in her throat. *Out of sight. Out of mind.* She slowly realized her affair with Sergio was infatuation born of loneliness, not real love.

Portly Sydney joined in, "Our court is well protected. Bill is a member of the Carmel police force. He's a relative newcomer."

Sydney, about her height and about twice her weight, contrasted so with Kyle that she immediately thought of the nursery rhyme, *Jack Sprat.* Jaden's eyes widened slightly in surprise. In Hal's rundown of the renters in the court, Bill's occupation really had not sunk in.

"Welcome to Carmel. I'm a newcomer, too. I've only been here about a year."

"Where are you from, Bill?"

"Transferred from Fresno. I could not resist the coast. It's beautiful."

"I think that's why I came, too. I even love those seagulls that I thought were barking dogs the first morning. I love their barking and the sound of the waves."

Had she ever been in love with Sergio? The truth jabbed at her. For a few seconds she lost track of the conversation. Jaden forced herself to listen to her dinner companions' conversation.

"It's really different here," Bill began.

"Certainly," Kyle said, chuckling. "His biggest collar was that woman who was stealing azaleas out of the planters in front of the Carmel Village Corner restaurant and the Village Gallery next door."

Except for Bill, everyone laughed. A muscle tightened at the corner of his mouth.

Jaden knew there was crime. She had been reading the Carmel Pine Cone that listed the police calls. Robbery was a big problem. All of their businesses had security alarms. Kyle told her that the year before someone stole a wooden carving of Father Serra in broad daylight from Gene at the California gallery in their court. One of a pair of thieves distracted him and the other one stole the statue. Insurance can't replace one-of-a-kind art objects.

"This apartment is just beautiful, Kyle and Sydney," Jaden complimented.

"Sydney's the decorator," Kyle admitted with his easy smile. "I know whatever he chooses will be just perfect. And expensive."

The large painting over the sofa of the famous lone cypress made the room look larger than Jaden's. As she stepped closer to the painting she almost thought she saw the waves surging. Jaden moved nearer. "The artist made the waves sparkle," she commented, trying to understand how he painted for that effect.

Bill moved to her side, "You like the scene?" he asked softly.

"Yes." Jaden thought she had seen the artist's work before, in Sergio's gallery.

"Aram," Sydney said with a huge smile. "You have good taste. They can be a wonderful investment, too, if you choose the right artist. But buy what you like, too."

"He uses a single name?" She made a mental note to return to the gallery. The restaurant must turn a profit because that artist's large paintings sold for $16,000.

"Some artists do," Bill told her, frowning, as though he disapproved.

"Many," Sydney added.

"He obviously loves the Monterey Bay area." Jaden sipped her drink.

Sydney commented, "This lone cypress is probably the most painted, photographed, and copied subject in California art and yet he's brought a fresh view to it."

"It's as though I were at the beach," Jaden commented. She felt a deep kinship with those ever restless, ever moving waves.

Esther, who had come in a few minutes earlier, moved to her side. "Impressionistic."

Her sparkling, clear blue eyes were set off by a light blue and pink flowered dress that fitted her beautifully. Her white hair framed the perfect oval of her wrinkled face.

"You know something about painting?"

"When I was a journalist, I traveled a lot. Museums and art galleries were always wonderful places to spend time when one did not know anybody in a foreign country."

"Bobbi," Esther asked, "Impressionist, don't you think? In spite of the traditional elements."

Bobbi smiled as she looked at the painting. "Yes, a wonderful example."

"The art in the library is beautiful and very valuable," Esther commented.

"Oh, yes. People are always asking about it. Many famous artists have donated to the library.

Both Harrison and the local history branch library have outstanding art."

This was the most Jaden had ever heard Bobbi say. She had to admire Esther's skill at drawing her out of her shell. Quiet people have a lot to say. Often they need a jump-start like turning the key in a music box.

"Dinner is served, everyone." Kyle lit the candles. "Please sit down. Jaden, Sydney, Hal, and I want to tell you about the open house for the cutlery shop."

Jaden lifted her glass as Sydney pronounced a toast. "Dinner for eight. May this be the first of many delightful gatherings."

Thanks to Kyle and Sydney she knew all of the apartment renters except the mystery man recluse, Mr. Emile Von Otto.

"I wish I could put a sign out in front of the shop," Jaden said the morning of the open house/ under new management party.

"Carmel is not big on signs," Hal answered with a smile. "The sign has been in the store window for three weeks, and, trust me, everyone knows about it. You know how every seagull for miles flocks to one crust of bread thrown on the beach? It will be like that. And we sent special invitations to the city employees, the mayor and city council and staff members."

Will Sergio come?

Jaden had now been in Carmel for almost nine weeks without a call or a sign from him. She felt more annoyed and angry with herself than with Sergio. Normally she had more sense. She dated casually. The slow dawn of reality told her that if Sergio had been a gunman in the old west he would have been constantly carving notches, not for kills, but for conquests. Being lonely does not excuse being stupid. Since Brent's death, Jaden knew that a part of her would always miss him. And, after all, Sergio had been mainly responsible for her move to this beautiful area.

The work of learning to run the store kept her completely occupied. For some reason being the new owner of "A Slice of Carmel" made her feel very connected to Grandpa Abel. A nice feeling. Jaden and Hal even spent time searching the internet for his knives.

Hal explained, "Now you can write off the cost of the knife as a business expense."

"With that kind of expense, the store will lose money," Jaden protested.

"Jaden," Hal broke in, "you will give the demonstration, won't you?"

"I don't know, Hal. What kind of a talent is knife throwing? Playing the piano is a talent."

"Your talent will discourage shoplifters," Hal answered with a laugh.

"O.K., but it's going to be short." She felt her face grow hot. "We had better make certain everyone is on the far opposite side of the court, though." She had practiced throwing the distance in the evenings after everything had closed. She could probably throw the knives blindfolded.

"I've got it all planned. Enrique will move everyone back for safety."

"Doesn't he look very elegant today?" she commented sincerely.

Kyle, in a tuxedo, was giving some last minute instructions to a tuxedoed Enrique and another man dressed the same way.

"Who is the other man?"

"I recognize him. He's a waiter at the Shell Game on Junipero."

Jaden knew she could not afford to walk into the Shell Game for a cup of coffee, although the restaurant's reputation was good. She might treat herself one day.

Sydney was bringing out trays of broiled shrimp when the first guests arrived.

Jaden recognized many of the chefs who visited to discuss knives and to have their own knives sharpened. Kyle served in his natural capacity as a greeter. Enrique and the waiter from the Shell Game bustled around with champagne and wine.

"What do you want to do about people like that?" Kyle asked her, pointing to a shaggy, gray-haired man wearing a backpack. Jaden recognized him as a homeless man who spent his days in the library and his nights who knew where.

"Just let him stay. This is an open party."

"There are a few more. They just aren't as obvious as Jonah," Kyle warned. "See that woman by Jonah? She goes to every funeral reception."

"As long as they behave themselves," Hal told him, "but have Enrique and your other employees keep a special eye on them. They will get them out a. s. a. p."

"Will do." Kyle turned to greet a woman with two toy poodles in tow. "Mrs. Van Dusen! And Sabrina and Greyling! So glad you could come!"

"I have to hold them," the woman confessed. "They'll want to beg."

I hope those two don't like shrimp, Jaden thought. Every morning a parade of dogs and their owners walked along the Carmel streets. Every breed in the world. The California gallery owner, Gene, kept a small box of dog bones by the door for the pooches.

Her eyebrows rose when she saw a white stretch limo pull up in front of the court and six people, three women and three men, emerged.

"It's the mayor and his wife with some friends," Hal whispered. "They love a grand appearance at any show."

A chef was asking Jaden to show him a particular knife that distracted her for a few minutes. "I'm going to buy that next week," he said. "Have you tried those prawns, Jaden? They taste sweet enough to be just pulled from the Sea of Cortez. And that cocktail sauce with horseradish. Magnificent! Nice party."

As he moved down the counter, Kyle and Hal walked into the store flanking a man who might be around fifty-five, dressed in a dark blue suit that fitted his broad shoulders very well. The woman who must be his wife was wearing a blue knitted cashmere suit that fit her perfectly, too. Jaden thought that suit would look elegant on Bobbi. Come to think of it, where was Bobbi?

Jaden had dragged her out to lunch at the Mad Hatter's one noon. The woman almost loosened up. Then she became guarded and even refused more walks to the beach.

"Jaden," Hal introduced the visitor, "I'd like you to meet Ted Rawlings, the mayor of Carmel, and his wife, Constance. Jaden Steele."

"So glad to meet you, Jaden." The man smiled and took her hand with a firm politician's grasp. "We've all been anxious to meet you. When Hal told me he planned to retire, we were worried that the cutlery shop would not continue. Do you have business experience?"

"No. I saw the Monterey Bay area last spring and decided that it would be a wonderful spot to live. When the business was up for sale on the internet, I decided to buy."

"We want to encourage business here," the mayor said, "especially women business owners. Do let me know if there's anything we can do to help with the store."

Run the shop at noon while I take a break? Buy some knives? She smiled thinking how unlikely that was. Constance had a job steering her husband. And she wore a suit that probably cost as much as one of Abel Cooper's knives from a designer, maybe *de Spain* or *Belle Noir*. The prices in the fashion magazines and the high end boutiques always made Jaden gulp.

Jaden said with a smile, "Thank you, Mayor Rawlings and Constance. Do you go by Constance or Connie?" She thought it was a natural question.

"My name is Constance," the mayor's wife answered, her lips tight. "Don't call me Connie."

The case of swords caught Ted's eye.

"Those are really somethin' special. A real attraction for your store. Ever sell any of them, Hal? And what's that little knife doin' in the case with the swords?"

"That's Jaden's grandfather's knife. A. Boxt. A is for Abel. He was one of the most famous crafters of handmade knives. That knife is worth about $1700. The price seems to go up every month. This case is our most secure one and that's why it's locked. We're negotiating for another Abel Cooper knife. "

"I'll be," Ted drawled with a soft southern accent. "If that little thing is $1700, how much are those swords?"

Jaden recognized the signs of someone who wanted to buy. She also saw that Constance was glaring at her husband and knew Ted would never own a sword.

"Ted, dear," she called in a sweet voice. "We have other people to meet."

Enrique moved up with a tray of champagne. Jaden, Constance, Ted, and Hal all took a glass. After the mayor's wife sipped, she asked Enrique, "My good man. Is there anything cooler?"

Enrique's eyes widened slightly and his face flushed. "Cooler?" he repeated.

Hal jumped in, "Más frío, Enrique, for Mrs. Rawlings. From the refrigerator."

Enrique nodded and melted into the crowd.

Constance said with a laugh, "Really, you can't make a silk purse...." Her friends laughed, too, along with the mayor's wife.

Jaden bit her lip. She lost respect for the Rawlings and their friends, who obviously laughed any time she made a joke, even at the expense of an innocent. They were like a gang of middle schoolers.

"Oh, Jaden," the mayor continued, "meet the city manager, Barton Collins, and my good friends, Marian and Sergio Martelli. Sergio is a city council member."

Jaden's mouth dropped open. She looked right past Marian into Sergio's dark eyes, feeling a jolt as though she had grabbed a wire with live current. He had enough grace to blush.

"I am so happy to meet you," Marian said. The fifty-ish woman was wearing a suit similar to the mayor's wife's, a pale yellow knitted top with matching pants. Jaden's eyes clouded for a moment. She felt her hands tremble and her face grow hot. Her voice caught in her throat and her eyes narrowed. She wanted to be anywhere else but here at this moment. She wanted to scream. Jaden did not know if she were angrier with Sergio or herself. In the back of her mind, she had already guessed something like this. *What a blind fool I was.*

"And my husband, Sergio," Marian took Sergio's arm in a possessive gesture.

He stepped forward slightly, and said, "Welcome to Carmel. Happy to meet you."

She clenched her fists so tightly that her nails were cutting into her palms.

Hal rescued her from herself.

"Jaden, Sergio. Excuse me." He took her aside, allowing her enough time to take some deep breaths. Her body trembled. She listened to her own heart drum in her ears. Was she angrier with him or herself for being so stupid?

"Lots of people are here now, Jaden. Would you please demonstrate your marvelous talent?" Hal asked.

She swallowed hard. Her mind raced to buy some time to steady her hands for knife throwing. Focus. *Focus.*

"Let me run upstairs for a minute…" she searched for an excuse, "and…and…where is Bobbi? I want to make sure she's O.K."

"That doesn't surprise me. She's not the social type. You know that."

"Still, she could come down for a while. Be right back." The stairs. She must get away.

Before Hal could answer, she turned and pushed her way to the stairs. She walked by Mr. Jonah, wolfing his prawns with accompanying pleasure grunts. *Someone's having a good time,* she thought as she ran up the steps, envying the man his temporary ecstasy.

She moved to Bobbi's door, the apartment next to hers, and knocked.

Jaden waited patiently, listening to Bobbi's footsteps come closer and closer to the door. It slowly opened. Peering around the side of the door, and without her glasses, Bobbi's eyes sparkled in an unusual golden hazel color with brown flecks. With a slight oriental shape they were beautiful. She suddenly reminded Jaden of some familiar movie or TV star. Who was it?

"Jaden. Why aren't you at your party?" She opened the door all the way.

"Why aren't you? Everyone else in town is. The library director. A lot of the employees. Politicians." *Would be great without Sergio.*

The starkness of the place surprised Jaden. No pictures on the walls. No framed portraits. No vases. Three books nestled next to a white ceramic lamp on the end table. She might just be moving in. This was so different from Kyle and Sydney's perfectly decorated apartment.

"I'm not dressed properly."

Without makeup and wearing a soft green exercise suit, Bobbi actually looked better than normal. In fact, she looked better than Constance Rawlings in her $1200 suit.

"Come down for a little while. The food is great. And…" she decided to brag, "I'm about to demonstrate my best talent."

"Really? What is it?"

"You'll have to come down and see. And I won't take no for an answer."

"Thank you, Jaden." Bobbi's smile lit up her face so that she looked actually happy for a few brief seconds. "Give me five minutes and I'll come." She closed the door.

Jaden moved to run into her apartment for a moment and bumped right into Sergio. He took her arm, "Jaden, my love, you don't know how I've missed you."

"Let me go!" She wrenched her arm away.

"I want to explain." Though he dropped his arms to his sides, his voice contained its usual seductive quality.

"You don't have to explain the obvious, Sergio. Please don't bother me." Her hands started to tremble. This time she knew it was with rage. Before she started any knife throwing, she had better gain control of herself and get rid of him.

"I want to see you again," he persisted. "Let me explain everything."

She must make him go away.

"If you'll go away right now!" she heard her voice rise.

"I will," his dark eyes peered into hers, "if you will see me later. You must, Jaden."

"All right! Just go away now!"

"Tonight. Midnight," he whispered in her ear. "In the parking garage below."

He turned and strolled down the stairs in front of Bobbi's room. He almost knocked over Mr. Jonah, who struggled to keep his footing.

"Hey!" the man yelled and began to mumble.

Jaden stared after Sergio. She felt her face pale with rage. *Midnight. You fool!*

Even worse, she saw Bobbi standing at her doorway with a puzzled look on her face. Below, next to the stairs, Bill and Kyle and some others were staring after Sergio. Jaden could not meet their eyes. She knew they must have heard at least some of what was said. Even Mr. Jonah, by the steps, had certainly heard the *Just go away.*

Jaden could not speak. *You'd better have the guts to tell Sergio to get lost.*

Bobbi, dressed in her sacky black suit that could double as a Halloween costume, closed the apartment door, and joined her. Kyle and Bill followed silently.

Hal spotted her coming down the steps and smiled. He clapped his hands together loudly. Everyone in the crowd turned toward him, "Ladies and gentlemen!"

He would have been a perfect ringmaster, Jaden thought. *Steady. Steady. Focus.*

"We have a special treat for you today." The crowd hushed to listen. "Jaden's grandfather was one of the country's most famous knife makers of the last century. He also was an expert knife thrower. And he taught his granddaughter both skills. I wish I had a drum roll. I talked her into this, believe me. Jaden Steele."

Adding to Jaden's embarrassment, the audience applauded. Samantha barked sharply until Mrs. Van Duren silenced her.

Hal held up a tray with the three familiar throwing knives. Murmurs moved through the crowd like waves. She and Hal had argued about the number to throw. Jaden won, refusing to prolong the demonstration beyond throwing the three. "It's dangerous enough."

"See the target set up on the wall over there," Hal pointed to the space between the arch leading to the stairs to the underground parking lot. "We've drawn a chalk line for safety. Please do not step over the line."

Enrique stood on one side of the court and the other waiter at the other side to watch for people who might stray over the line. There was always someone who had not heard or did not think that request was meant for them.

The court, filled with noisy conversations only moments before, became quiet.

Hal offered her the tray.

She took the knife. The feel of the handle brought back her grandfather's voice.

"Jaden, nothing exists except for you and the target. Clear your mind."

The hours and hours of practice returned to her. She had practiced with them at night when only Hal was with her. Jaden made certain the handle weights were perfect.

She flexed her knees and stepped forward slightly with her left foot. Her first throw propelled directly to the center of the target. The audience applauded. The second went slightly to the right of the first. The applause and murmurs distracted her until she forced them to fade. She lifted the last knife with her right hand. Her throw flew straight to the center and dislodged the first knife and bit into the center of the target.

The applause brought Jaden back from her deep concentration.

While everyone else was applauding, Bobbi, who had been standing next to Bill, whirled and ran up the steps to her apartment. The door closed.

Jaden knew that was the last they would see of her today. *Did I frighten her?* She almost felt worse about Bobbi than Sergio. Jaden already planned to tell him what she thought about him in terms even he would understand. No swearing. No shouting. He would never touch her again. She was coming late to wisdom, but better late than never.

Trying to bridge the gap of loneliness in her life, Jaden had made one big mistake that she swore she would never be repeated.

The first person to shake her hand with his warm bear paws was Rawlings. "That was great! Don't lose that talent, little lady. Ain't many that have it." The little drawl was maybe Texas. Maybe a Texas millionaire. Constance would look for money to marry. Could be the reverse, though. The mayor's wife was unusually harsh. A Yankee.

Jaden, shame on you. Angry thoughts buzzed around her like mosquitoes.

People in the crowd pressed around her with congratulations. She noticed everyone except Marian and Sergio Martelli. They must have left right after the demonstration because they were gone. Had Marian noticed his little jaunt up the steps? A number of people must have heard her.

By six o'clock exhaustion was consuming Jaden. Most of the crowd was gone and about a dozen of them sat around two of the tables in the courtyard. She saw Enrique in the kitchen of The Mad Hatter's, removing dishes from the dishwasher and placing them carefully in the cupboards that lined one side of the small café's walls. Sydney and Kyle brought a last tray of the most delicious creamy cream cheese Jaden had ever tasted, a tray of crackers, and a tray of carrots, radishes, broccoli, kohlrabi, and sweet cherry tomatoes.

Esther, the only one of the group who did not appear tired, asked, "Where do you buy this cream cheese? And another glass of that champagne would be wonderful."

"It comes from Hilmar Cheese Factory over in the valley," Sydney told them.

"Finish up," Kyle ordered. We can't leave the champagne to go flat, either. He brought a chair up next to Jaden. "Could I tell you something?" he asked quietly.

"Kyle, Sydney, the food was wonderful. Thank you so much. Your catering was the best part of this strange day."

"You are welcome," Sydney said with a bow, almost puffing up with the compliment.

"Can you order me some of this cream cheese?" Amanda Perkins, the library director, was asking, engaging Sydney on the virtues of proper purchasing of food.

Kyle leaned close to Jaden. "That man…."

He did not have to explain what Jaden already knew, but she kept quiet.

"He's not worth your time."

She choked out, "He's a womanizer. I know that, Kyle. Thank you, though."

"It's well known. I decided to risk your getting mad at me for the news."

Jaden's eyes brimmed with angry tears. "Is there any more of that champagne, Kyle?"

She downed two glasses in a matter of minutes. Trouble started when she tried to stand up. The court whirled. Bill moved to her. His muscular arm slipped under her shoulder and behind her back. She regained her balance just as Hal came out of the shop.

"Kyle," he said with a slight frown on his forehead. "One of the knives that was on the black tray is missing. Must have fallen."

"We'll search the court and the garbage. That's where some utensils end up by accident." The remaining group began to search under the tables and in the planters.

Jaden found she could not look down without the world spinning. "Maybe someone was curious and just wanted to look at it."

"Or maybe someone stole it," Hal said bitterly. "It's my fault. We could easily have lost more, too. I was not paying enough attention. I'm going to check the shop."

No way could Jaden help him search. "I'm sorry, Hal. I have to go upstairs."

"Let me help you," Esther offered.

Helped by an almost 87-year-old woman.

She angled her way up the stairs with Esther supporting her by one arm. She felt someone behind her and did not realize it was Bill until they reached the door of her apartment. He stood right behind her, probably to catch her if she fell.

Esther said, "Key, Jaden?" Jaden slipped the key from the pocket of her jacket.

"Do you need any help?" Bill's voice plowed into her now pounding head.

"No. Thank you both, very much."

When the door closed, she propelled herself to the bedroom and dived into the bed. Head spinning, stomach turning, she set the clock for 11:45 p.m. to meet Sergio at midnight.

.

The shrill alarm woke Jaden. When she tried to sit up, her head spun like a speeding carousel.

She would have to make the bathroom quickly, even if she had to crawl every inch on her shaky knees.

Her stomach heaved. She staggered to the bathroom just in time.

I want to die. She wiped her face with a cold, wet washcloth. Turning on the sixty watt bathroom light blinded her for a few seconds. When her vision cleared, she looked in the mirror.

A groan issued from her cracked lips.

"This hellish sight ought to discourage Lover Boy." Groaning with each movement, Jaden slipped into her blue exercise suit.

The clock beeped its second warning, just in case the poor sleeping body had not heard the first time. She ran over to depress the button and blinked. The time read,

"Twelve fifty-five!"

Her foggy memory of setting the alarm jumped up and down in the back of her mind. Maybe she set it wrong deliberately to avoid seeing him. Whatever, he must have left by now. She mumbled to herself like Mr. Jonah.

This would only prolong what should have been settled an hour ago. Stomach still protesting and queasy, head pounding, she forced herself to dash for the door.

What in the...her neighbor's lights, she counted three, were still on. The living room light was on at Bobbi's, the living room and bedroom at Kyle and Sydney's, and a light was on in Bill's bedroom. Only Esther's apartment was dark. Jaden's mouth dropped open. *Four of them.* There was even a light on at Emile Von Otto's.

Overwhelming curiosity, one of her worst traits, was tempting her to knock on that door. "I've never been out this late," she muttered to herself. "Don't know much about them. Maybe they're all night owls." Resisting that temptation, Jaden walked down the stairs and down to the court, across the flagstones to the entrance to the parking garage in the alleyway between the shop and the California Gallery. She heard a loud snort, and noticed a lumpy form leaning against the alley wall by the dryer vent.

Sergio? No. It was the homeless man, Jonah. She did not pause. If she woke him, there might be an unwanted confrontation. Her hand automatically pulled the Monarch from her pocket. Jaden quickly tested the torsion blade. She closed the knife and slipped it back into her pocket. She continued to walk to the light.

The light was on at the top of the stairs to the parking garage, but the garage was dark. "That's funny. I thought that was always on in the garage for security, but I've never been here this late. Maybe it's on a timer."

She descended slowly, moving more and more into the dimness of the garage. Five cars were parked in the space for seven. Bill's, hers, Bobbi's, and Kyle's and Sydney's. A funny odor drifted to her nostrils. Must be the dumpster, overloaded with garbage from the open house, and the washer and dryer for the complex were in alcoves on either side of the concrete stairs.

"Sergio?" her voice wavered. "Are you still here?" She turned the switch on for the dumpster alcove and left it on to be able to see. The laundry room next to the dumpster was the only place left. He must have gone, but she would look. Her tennis shoes felt wet. Jaden stared down at a dark pool. "The washer must have leaked."

She gasped. A man's figure sat on the plastic chair next to the small table used to fold clothes.

Jaden flicked on the light.

She knew that smell now. Blood. She was standing in a puddle of blood.

Sergio's blood.

Sergio Martelli was slumped in a chair with the handle of one of A Slice of Carmel's best kitchen knives protruding from his beautiful dark silk sports coat. From five feet away Jaden knew he was dead.

A wave of nausea swept over her. Her stomach was still churning from being sick in her apartment. Head whirling, she clutched the door frame to steady herself. A scream trapped itself somewhere in her chest. Her heart pounded irregularly, like a drum gone crazy. The scream suddenly burst from her throat.

Call 911. There's a phone down here somewhere. She found it on the wall by the entrance/exit to the street. A pay phone, naturally. She knew one credit card number by heart. Jaden thought you were supposed to be able to call emergency without money. She could not wait. With trembling hands she pressed 911.

"Jaden, you don't have to work in the store today. You must have been up most of the night," Hal said as he unlocked the front door and keyed in the disarming code for the security system.

"It's better that I work, Hal," she answered, her head still aching dully. She needed sleep but there was no way she could have slept last night.

"Do you have any relatives you can call?"

Jaden shook her head. No relatives. That fact hit her like one of her throwing knives hitting the target. A wave of self-pity that she quickly dismissed was replaced with a deep pang of guilt.

She should be feeling sorry for Sergio and his relatives. His wife.

"The police took Mr. Jonah away last night," Jaden told him.

"Bill told me that they asked Bobbi Jones to come in for questioning."

"Bobbi? Why on earth? Bobbi didn't know Sergio. She did not have a chance to steal that knife, either." Jaden slowly drew a knife that had been left by the chef of The Shell Game down one of the sharpening files. Chefs despised dull knives. She tried to clear away all the confused thoughts in her mind. *Not Bobbi!* Did Sergio make a pass at Bobbi? Or had an affair with her, too? *Impossible.* She tested the blade with her thumb instead of the right way, with a piece of paper. Sharp. The slice bit into her thumb and started to bleed immediately. Jaden stared at the blood. *More blood. Too much blood.* She gagged.

Finally Jaden ran to the bathroom to press the wound until the bleeding stopped. She put on a bandage and returned to knife sharpening. Around two p.m. she saw Bobbi return from the police interview accompanied by a tall blond man in a dark suit. They sat down at one of the Mad Hatter's outdoor tables.

"Hal." Jaden put down the second now very sharp knife she had been honing.

"I want to talk to Bobbi for a minute."

He nodded as Jaden walked out the door toward Bobbi and the stranger.

"Bobbi," she asked, "Are you all right?"

Her friend stared at her with a pale face. "Thank you, Jaden. Oh, I'd like to introduce you to McKenzie Anderson. McKenzie is…" her voice faltered and she sighed.

The man stood up and pulled out a chair for Jaden. "Won't you sit down? I'm Bobbi's attorney and a friend."

Lawyer? Handsome with great manners. Jaden felt as though she knew this man. How could it be possible that he seemed familiar?

"We were going to have some coffee." The man asked, "Please join us."

"Thank you," Jaden said. "This is the best coffee in Carmel-by-the-sea."

"McKenzie is my attorney," Bobbi explained.

"They can't suspect you? The murder weapon was a knife from our store. Hal discovered two knives and a throwing knife were missing."

"I'm certain you will be called in. If you need an attorney, I'm as good an ambulance chaser as anyone else." McKenzie handed her a card. His office was in San Diego. Now why in the world would Bobbi call a lawyer from San Diego? Jaden knew her mouth dropped open. She deliberately clamped it shut. Something about the two of them suddenly triggered a vivid memory in Jaden's mind. She *had* seen him before. And Bobbi, too.

Jaden closed her eyes. A black and white picture from the newspaper popped into her mind. McKenzie was there, attempting to shield his woman client from what must have been a hundred cameras. Her eyes opened and she stared at Bobbi. A low moan gurgled in her throat.

Bobbi was asking, "Would you like some iced tea or coffee, Jaden? You look like you need rest. I can't tell you how awful I feel about Sergio, especially since, my..."

Her voice deserted her. McKenzie patted her hand sympathetically.

"Why would they call you in for questioning? You did not even know him."

Bobbi stared over her shoulder into some other place "But I am a suspect."

Jaden's face hardened as she stared at the woman. *Suspect. Suspect.*

McKenzie's large hand took Bobbi's. "You don't have to say more."

"Jaden at least deserves an explanation." She set down her steaming mug. "My full name is Petra Roberta Jones-Schmidt."

Jaden clutched the arm of the plastic chair. This woman had been the most famous person in the country for the first six months of last year. People who did not know who the vice-president was knew her. You could not buy groceries without seeing her face at checkout in every tabloid newspaper. Sick headlines like, *Did Petra's Boyfriend Make Her Kill? Or, Petra's Affairs Enrage Hubby.* Television shows reviewed the trial constantly. Every moment of her life had been reviewed and re-reviewed in every form of media. Each paper tried to outdo the other with rumor mongering and scandal. This year she was old news. She might have dropped off the edge of the world.

"To be perfectly honest, I needed a place to hide," Petra-Bobbi continued. "My best friend from school is Amanda Perkins, the library director here. She suggested this little tourist town where no one would pay attention to me. I changed my appearance as much as possible and kept to myself. How was I to know that tragedy would strike here? I swear to you, Jaden, I had nothing to do with this. I must find a way to clear myself. I don't want that nightmare to come back!" She covered her face with her hands.

Jaden said quietly, "I believe you." If Bobbi murdered someone here after everything she went through, she would have to be the world's biggest idiot. And Jaden knew she was a highly intelligent woman. Jaden also sympathized with Petra's need to start a new life. The last thing the woman would want would be more publicity.

McKenzie told her, "Petra, you are innocent until proven guilty."

"Under the law," she answered. "Not in some people's minds. McKenzie, I am never going to be free of suspicion no matter what I do or where I go! I needed this new life."

Jaden glanced up to see Bill Amirkhanian enter Dolores Court with another police officer. They were walking straight for their table.

"McKenzie," she gulped her iced tea.

"I believe I may need your services."

How ridiculous to be more worried about the price of one of the country's most famous attorneys than about her own skin.

Jaden, you wanted a change and you got it.

Murphy's law was operating at full speed in the village of Carmel-by-the-sea.

McKenzie spoke to her alone briefly. "Be as honest as you can. And just answer the questions. Don't volunteer anything. I've not had time to review the events of last night. I'll have to return to San Diego soon. We'll arrange a time for me to get all the facts. You knew the victim?"

She looked down and nodded.

"You dated him?"

"About four times on that one weekend."

"You had an affair with him?

Her face burned. "Yes."

McKenzie groaned.

At least he had the grace not to mention how foolish she had been.

"I did not kill him! As soon as I found out he was married, I planned to tell him to get out of my life. In fact, I tried to tell him when he followed me upstairs. How could anyone think I would kill him right in our own parking garage? With a knife from my store?"

"I believe you and I believe Petra. That woman never should have been prosecuted but she was. Right now it's not what I believe that's important. It's what the police believe."

She sat at the small table in a bare room at the Carmel police station. Jaden could not imagine answering these questions without McKenzie there. In the room was a policewoman taking notes, Bill, and the police chief.

The police chief began, "When did you meet Sergio Martelli, Mrs. Steele?"

"At Asilomar, the first weekend of April."

"You dated him?"

"Yes."

"Did you have an affair with him?"

Jaden looked at McKenzie but could not look at Bill. "Yes." She was barely able to say that.

"You moved to Carmel to be with him?"

She looked pleadingly at McKenzie, who nodded. "I thought so at first," she began, "but then I realized how much I wanted a change in my life." She heard her voice waver. "Everything at home in Nebraska reminded me of my husband, Brent, and my grandparents who raised me."

"He died?"

The question sounded so suspicious that she glared up at him. They could not possibly think that she killed Brent? "He was killed by a drunk driver a year ago."

She felt her face grow hot, and, in spite of herself, her eyes brimmed with tears.

Bill broke in, "Would you like some water?" His eyes seemed to darken to blacker.

"Thank you," she answered, clearing her throat. "I'd like that."

McKenzie broke in, "Let's resume this later."

Jaden shook her head. She wanted to get this over. Her head was pounding and she desperately needed sleep. "No. I'm O.K." *What a lie.*

The chief persisted, "You came to Carmel to resume the affair?"

"No," came a half-truth. "The first time I saw Sergio again was at the party yesterday."

"You met Mrs. Martelli?"

"Yes, but...I had already realized how unhappy and vulnerable I was after my husband's death. What I really wanted was a change in my life. It helped to come to a different environment."

"A change?" his eyebrows went up.

"Didn't take much intuition to realize something or someone kept Sergio from contacting me for over two months. Obvious that something was wrong."

"You found out suddenly that he was married. You were angry."

"Of course. No. Wait… more with myself."

She noticed a flicker of a smile cross Bill's face and quickly disappear.

"You still agreed to meet this man in the middle of the night? You thought you could resume the affair?"

"No!"

McKenzie cleared his throat.

Jaden shook her head. "He insisted. I told him to go away. Sergio promised he would if I would meet him in the garage. I wanted nothing more to do with him."

"He was a liar and a cheat and he really made you angry when you found out."

McKenzie interrupted, "You are putting words into my client's mouth."

"O.K. O.K. Mrs. Steele, you are an expert with knives, is that correct?"

"I'm not sure what you mean. I own a cutlery store. My grandfather taught me to throw knives."

"We understand you are an expert."

McKenzie broke in. "That's enough for today. I need to confer with my client."

Jaden realized that of course he did not know about her "talent." Her head pounded and she felt sick to her stomach. She knew the color was draining from her face.

McKenzie walked her home.

"I could not have taken that another minute. Thank you so much."

"Part of my job, ma'am. Jaden, we're going to have to arrange an appointment next week and we'll go over everything minute by minute. I know you don't feel well now. And tell me about the knife throwing. If you can possibly write down what you remember that will help."

Bobbi and Hal met them as they walked into the courtyard. Bobbi put her arm over Jaden's shoulder. "I'm so sorry about all of this."

Hal commented, "You look like you need to get to bed."

Jaden nodded. She could not even talk.

"It's awful. Those interviews. I still have nightmares," Bobbi took her arm.

"I mean…when you know you are telling the truth and people don't believe," her famous, or infamous neighbor continued. "It's so frustrating when you know they want someone to be guilty. You tell the truth and they twist your words…."

Hal said, "Let's get Jaden upstairs."

She managed the stairs on her own, entered her apartment and flopped on the bed.

Bobbi covered her with a light blanket.

At first, Jaden thought her mind would not halt its spinning and her eyes would not close.

The position of her body did not change the whole time she was asleep. A loud drumming was the only reason she woke into a groggy fog. Her vision blurred.

She blinked at the clock.

Four-thirty in the afternoon!

The noise was a pounding at the door. She rose slowly and headed for the living room. Hal and Kyle stood in the doorway.

"Oh, Hal, I'm so sorry! The shop."

"That's all right. I knew you had to sleep. We're checking on you. Sorry we woke you."

"I brought you some chowder," Kyle set a white quart container on the sink. The aroma from the soup drifted into her nostrils. Sydney made the most delicious chowder in the world. Her stomach was growling. The last time she ate was yesterday around noon.

"Sit down," she said.

Hal and Kyle sat down at the round oak table that had belonged to her grandparents. "The phone's been ringing off the hook," Hal told her. "Reporters. I've told them that you are not available indefinitely."

"Thank you, Hal. McKenzie told me not to speak to anyone. Some time next week he's coming back. I need some coffee." Her hands shook trying to press the button on the coffee grinder. She finally managed to scoop coffee into the filter and fill the small pot with water.

"Sit down, Jaden," Kyle said quietly but firmly. "When it's ready I'll pour."

"Hal, Kyle, did they tell you about Bobbi?"

"All I knew was there was something strange about her coming here."

"That's what I thought, too," Hal added.

"Strange?"

"Bobbi didn't rent the apartment. Amanda Perkins and Bill arranged the first year's lease. If that were not unusual enough, her acting like a hermit made me suspicious. At first I thought she was one of those people who is afraid of going outside. She went to work, went to the market, and was pleasant enough when I talked to her.

67

Answers were always so short, usually a few words, if that."

"She was trying to escape all that horrible publicity. Now this."

Kyle said, "To sell papers they print unfounded rumors. They're like sharks that smell blood. A gash or open wound. No difference. Whether it's true or not true."

Jaden almost gagged remembering the pungent blood smell in the garage.

The sight of Sergio dead might never leave her mind. Her grandmother and her grandfather were always believers in fate. *Everything happens for a reason, Jaden. You recovered from the flu that took your parents for a reason. Your time is not up yet.* Your life had a plan. If that were the truth, you should know what it was. If this were her plan, she was in trouble.

"Eat some of the soup, Jaden. You will feel better with something in your stomach." Kyle put the spoon handle in her hand. He probably would have spoon fed her if she had not lifted the spoon into the steaming bowl.

"This is delicious," Jaden commented between sips of the creamy clam chowder.

"Five-ninety five plus tax per quart," Kyle answered with a grin. "It's Sydney's specialty. Loaded with clams. It's one of our most popular take-out items."

She thought her heart was slowing down. "My stomach is feeling better. Thank you."

"Finding Sergio like that was a big shock," Hal commented.

"I'll never forget. Have they questioned you, yet?" Jaden asked.

"No, I said I wanted my attorney to come from San Jose. My turn is tomorrow. Luckily I was at Sandy's near Fourth Street and San Carlos. Been staying there."

"You have an alibi," Kyle poured the coffee into a mug and offered it to Jaden.

"Sydney and I can alibi each other. You and Bobbi and Esther and Bill are the ones who don't have alibis."

"Von Otto was here," Jaden told them.

Kyle and Hal both stared at her.

"There were lights on in his apartment, Bobbi's, and Bill's. The others were dark."

"I'll be," Hal said. "Beats me how Von Otto sneaks in and out."

"Then he must have come in or out about the time of the murder," Kyle said.

"You're right," Hal insisted. "The police need to know. Let's see if they can meet him."

On the computer Petra entered the name William Amirkhanian in the Census records for 1970. A string of Amirkhanians came up but no Bill or William. *1980. Same thing.* She guessed his age as middle 30's. He should be in the 1980 census. She took the time to look at the A's one by one. Aram Amirkhanian. She looked for California records. Aram Amirkhanian was the correct age. B. 1979. Father ARAM. Mother Sylvia. They moved to Fresno from New York.

Birth records. There it was. Aram William Amirkhanian. She gasped. Bill had a secret that she would tell Jaden this evening. Most of the people she knew, including Jaden, were attending Sergio Martelli's funeral. *I'll look up Jaden.* Though she liked the owner of A Slice of Carmel, she could not rule out the woman who had both motive, opportunity, and a talent with knives. Petra shivered. She could not bring herself to buy a kitchen knife. Would she have moved here if she had known the apartment was near a cutlery store?

Jaden Steele. Nebraska. Parents Mary and Abel died in the same week when their daughter was only seven years old. The woman was exactly who she said she was. Petra printed out the information about Bill to show Jaden as soon as possible. She could understand why he might want to keep his art separate from his police work.

Mourners filled the beautiful Carmel Mission Church for the Catholic funeral mass. During the long service, the bird songs that filled the air of the mission garden proved distracting. The birds obviously did not comprehend the sad occasion.

Trying to sense the killer, Jaden made herself look at each person at the service who could be involved in the murder. Constance and Ted Rawlings sat next to Marian Martelli on one side. A woman who sat on the other side looked so much like Marian that she must be a sister. Although they were never introduced, Jaden remembered her from the open house at Dolores Street Court. Vincent Howard sat next to her. Jaden listened to a series of strangers telling their memories of Sergio. She closed her eyes.

I learned a lot from Sergio. Number One was to never repeat my mistake.

After the mass, she rode in Kyle and Sydney's old Lincoln to the Seventeen-Mile Drive home of Abby Wilson, Marian Martelli's sister. The two were staying close to her on purpose. She could not have made herself attend without them. Sandy and Hal had also invited her. Esther came with them. She did not see Bill or Bobbi in the chapel crowd.

Once inside the home they paid their respects to the distraught widow. Jaden could not look the woman in the eyes. No one seemed to remember, or possibly they were too polite to mention that Jaden had discovered the body. The police had also questioned her. Though police activities should be confidential, the mayor would probably have kept in contact with the police, especially since Sergio was on the city council. The murder was front page news in every local paper.

"Who do you think prepared this food?" Sydney asked quietly, nibbling on a thin slice of pressed ham.

Kyle's eyebrows went up and he grimaced. "In spite of those iceberg lettuce leaves added for garnish you can see the cheese and crackers and sliced meats are all on those supermarket trays. The least someone could have done was transfer the fare to real china or silver platters."

"Meow," Sydney said with a chuckle.

Kyle grinned. "I'm going to have a drink. May I bring you one, Jaden?"

"Thank you, Kyle. Cabernet or Merlot if they have it." She almost said, *A large glass.*

"They will." He left and Sydney started a conversation with Vincent.

Kyle returned and handed her the glass of deep burgundy wine, "Cabernet. From a huge, generic bottle. Are you all right? I wanted to speak to the Rawlings for a moment. It's about catering a party at their home."

"I'll be fine. Go ahead."

She noticed Abby Wilson standing by herself and went over. "I am so sorry," she told the woman, who had a deep pink nose from crying.

Abby did not respond, except to say, "Thank you for coming. I need some fresh air. Would you like to go out on the balcony?"

Jaden nodded. She followed Abby out the French doors to the ocean side balcony.

"What a gorgeous view of the whole bay. How long have you lived here?"

"Marian and I were raised in this house. This was our home. When Marian married Sergio…" she cleared her throat and turned to stare out to the Pacific Ocean.

Jaden kept quiet.

"My husband and I bought out Marian. At first, she was so happy with Sergio."

"I haven't met your husband." Jaden knew immediately something was wrong and wished she could take back the words.

"Died of cancer," Abby explained quietly. "Marian and even Sergio were such a help during those terrible months. Sergio was never mean during that time. Completely thoughtful."

"I'm so sorry. I'm a widow, too." Tears burned in Jaden's eyes.

"Oh, but you are so young."

"I didn't have any relatives to help me."

"Marian was wonderful. Sergio, well, Sergio and I had our disagreements."

Jaden guessed before Abby said, "I tried to talk to him about…."

Wasn't hard to guess the problem.

"Did you know Sergio?" Abby's drink was emptied in one huge gulp.

Guilt made Jaden think, *Beam me up, Scotty. If only I could disappear right now.*

"Marian wanted that womanizer Sergio no matter what he did. I never understood it. She deserved better. He was the one subject that came between us. She would not listen to me. Love is really blind. He went through her money like water through a sieve. And he imagined himself the world's greatest lover. My sister will never realize that whoever killed him did her a big favor." Her face was pink. Her words were slurred or Jaden would never have heard such an opinion.

"I am very sorry," were the only words she could say with complete sincerity.

Kyle's tall frame appeared in the doorway. "Jaden, we should be leaving."

"Of course, Kyle."

He moved over to hug Abby, "My dear, I am so sorry about your brother-in-law."

A small sigh escaped Abby's lips and she turned away from him toward the ocean. "Thank you." The quiet words drifted off in the slight breeze off the Pacific.

Abby followed them from the deck and headed straight for the bar.

As they walked quietly to Kyle's dark blue Lincoln, Jaden wished she could have tape-recorded that conversation. She would make notes as soon as she got home. The list of those who might have wanted Sergio dead was probably as endless as the heavens.

Once in the car, Sydney said excitedly, "Wait until you hear about my conversation with Sergio's partner, Vincent!"

Jaden, who was sitting on the passenger's side of the front seat, turned back toward him.

Sydney's sea green eyes blazed under his shiny balding forehead fringed by a thin frosting of red hair. "Do you remember that beautiful art work that is on display at Harrison Library?"

"The art that has been donated to the library over the years for the people to enjoy?" she said.

Kyle answered. "Carmel has always been a haven for artists since the Bohemian days early in the twentieth century," he explained to Jaden.

"Sergio proposed secretly to the mayor that the city sell the works of art."

"That does not make sense. The art is valuable although it won't raise huge amounts of money. It would be a short term gain for a huge long term loss." Kyle shook his head.

"Not for Sergio. He would have profited by being the agent. Vincent realized he was appraising the art pieces, and asked him. That's why he knew about the proposal."

"Sergio stormed back to the gallery one day fuming because the mayor, to his credit, absolutely refused. Sergio blabbed to Vincent and said the mayor was, well, you can guess. Rawlings told him that the library had suffered enough from the budget cuts and he was elected as a reform mayor. They were not going to sell the donated art work."

"Would the sale have been legal?" Kyle asked with a frown.

"You know the old bunch did everything arbitrarily. They did not care what happened and had some lame explanation later. Sergio was part of that group. If the sale were quick and made a profit, he figured no one would say a word. They could get rid of any employee who complained by one excuse or another. Typical. Power corrupts. People like that want more and more power."

Jaden groaned. "How could I ever have gotten mixed up with Sergio? There was larceny under that world's greatest lover façade. He did not have a conscience."

"Right. He was a practiced charmer," Kyle responded. "You were not alone."

Sydney continued, "I understand Mayor Rawlings told Sergio, 'We'll have to find somewhere else to cut. I was elected with the promise to improve the library, to restore services, and that's what I'm going to do. And I'm never going to wink at actions that I know are wrong!' My friend said that Sergio stormed out. I'm on the library board and never heard a word of this. I would have been furious. What a rotten idea."

"I'm astonished," Kyle pulled down the driver's visor to press the remote to open the gate of the parking garage. "A politician who actually turned down easy money. He ought to have his own museum. See the political dinosaur."

Jaden's mouth went dry. She put her trembling hand on the car door handle.

"Kyle, would you let me out?"

"I'm sorry, Jaden." He stopped the car.

Heart thundering, Jaden swung her feet to the sidewalk. She gulped in a deep breath of fresh air, not knowing if she could ever go into the parking garage again.

Jaden's feet barely moved one after the other up the concrete steps. Her muscles ached and her mind whirled. She wanted to flop into bed to sleep for about twenty-four hours but she forced herself to sit at her old battered oak desk, a prized possession of her Grandpa Abel's. When she rubbed the scarred oak top, she felt close to Grandpa. He was so much like a father to her. She could close her eyes and see him concentrating deeply on his bookwork.

With a sigh she opened her tired eyes, pulled out a notebook from a desk drawer, and started to write down everything she remembered from the service and from the gathering afterward. Marian's sister, Abby, the sister who did not like Sergio, was easily added to Jaden's growing list of suspects.

What had Jaden seen? What had she heard? Abby was no fan of Sergio. Write down every little detail, no matter how small. Sergio was not above larceny. He was dishonest and cheated on Marian continually.

How could I ever have fallen for him?

Marian was very unlikely to have murdered her husband. She wanted him for her own status no matter what he did. The man knew it. He did not need to change his behavior to keep her. Unless a sudden fit of jealousy made her temporarily insane….

"She could have followed him that night," Jaden muttered to herself.

People from the open house, she wrote, *people who could have heard Sergio talking to me. Who had motives?*

Her list was getting longer instead of shorter.

She added Amanda Perkins. "That art work was a new twist. After all the budget cuts to the small library including the ultimate ridiculous economy, the layoff of the janitors, the thought of losing the beautiful art might have pushed her over the edge. The city council did not understand the value to the community of library services." Bobbi, or Petra, certainly heard Sergio's words. She was the one person Jaden did not suspect. She would have to be a fool to do anything wrong after what had happened to her. Unless she was insane, Bobbi was no fool. "She could have told Amanda, though."

Jaden groaned. *Talking to oneself is not a good sign.*

A knock at the door made her heart race.

Her grandparent's old Seth Thomas clock on the mantle chimed eight o'clock.

Jaden stood up and moved to the door. She opened it warily. Bobbi stood there with a folder in her arms. Jaden was too tired to worry about whether or not she was inviting an insane serial killer into her apartment.

"Bobbi, come in." Once she closed the door she asked, "Would you rather I call you Petra? I was just going to make some tea. Join me, please, or would you rather have coffee?"

"Tea is fine, thank you. It's best to stay with calling me Bobbi, I think." She put her folder on the sofa. "I've been doing some computer research, person by person. These are my notes."

"I can't rule out anyone yet," Jaden told her as she brought out the box with the tea and sugar. From the refrigerator she took a quart carton of milk. She thought of lemon, but a sudden chill made her unwilling to draw out a knife in front of Bobbi. *No knife. She would never deliberately use a knife in the woman's presence.* Still, she was not afraid of Bobbi/Petra. From the first time they met, Jaden was intrigued. Her instincts were usually correct.

And at this point she needed to trust someone. She liked her neighbor.

Bobbi said, "This is what I have learned so far. Everyone is who he says he is except for what I believe about Bill."

"Bill?"

"1980 census. I think his first name is Aram."

Jaden stared at her. "Aram? You mean…?"

"He may not have moved here just to join the police department. Aram is a fairly common Armenian name. Tomorrow I'll go to the library early and try again."

Aram, Jaden thought. She remembered seeing his apartment light on late at night. Could he be working with an artistic frenzy late into the night? Something told her that her guess might be true. *Bobbi is highly intelligent. She would never stab someone so close to her own apartment. Who would be number one on the suspect list?*

"Bobbi, could anyone have guessed your identity before the murder?"

"I suppose it's possible. Amanda Perkins knew. Since she has been my friend since college I'm positive she would not say anything. The police knew. My identity was to be a secret, but people sometimes slip. Mayor Rawlings may have been informed by someone in the police department who wanted to protect himself. Jaden, I must clear myself. I'll never be free. Trouble seems to follow me whatever I do."

"I just wondered. Someone who knew might have seized the chance to throw suspicion on you, and, by the way, on me."

"Someone who knew you had been involved with Sergio. Someone who also knew about the midnight appointment that he planned with you."

"Let's write them down." Jaden began her list with "*Me*. I am the most obvious. Why would you kill Sergio?"

"I was at my door. I heard almost every word when he cornered you. So did Hal and Bill. I'm sure of that, and that group at the bottom of the open steps. Sergio almost knocked over Jonah at the bottom of the concrete steps."

"Enrique, Amanda...." Jaden closed her eyes. There were more. At least ten people congregated at the bottom of the steps. "I was so upset at the time. Some tall men... Kyle, and Ted Rawlings!" She rested her left hand against her forehead. "Kyle warned me about Sergio later. I'm sure he knew. He was so kind and cautious about approaching me with his advice."

"Esther," Bobbi mentioned. "She does not miss a thing. Vincent, trying to charm Abby. I don't think Marian was there. Abby might have told her."

"Did everyone in town know about me and Sergio?" Jaden asked with a groan.

"Carmel is like a small town in fancy dress."

"Bobbi, did you know about Sergio's plan to sell the library's art holdings?"

The librarian looked shocked. "Sell the paintings? How could they?"

"According to Sydney, the way they did everything else. Do it first and then apologize later if caught."

"The library board would have to protest but would they have any power?"

"The city attorney would represent city hall. The board would be powerless unless they hired an attorney and who would pay? They don't have the funds for legal fees."

"Sergio wanted to handle the sales."

"How could he ethically do that?" Bobbi wondered aloud. "Ethics were not his long suit."

"Ethics were not high on Sergio's list of behaviors. Work secretly and if anyone said anything make some excuse. Mayor Rawlings opposed the plan. He told Sergio he meant to keep his promises and the art. Some of the council members who did not understand the circumstances thought it was a great fundraising plan. Most of them sided with the mayor."

"So a political storm was brewing."

"Rawlings called Sergio greedy, according to several of Sydney's sources."

Bobbi commented, "Sydney usually gets his facts straight. And he knows art."

Jaden thought that the city politics must be like the sea. Maybe smooth on the surface but ever moving and always dangerous. A misstep and those treacherous waves in the form of people or media would pull you down.

"Bobbi, I'll make copies of these notes and your research if it's all right with you. We'll each have a copy of the notes and we may find something that will seem odd."

"Out of the ordinary?" Bobbi sipped her tea.

"In the meantime, I'm continuing to talk to people about Sergio informally. See what I can glean. My best suspect is still the homeless man, Mr. Jonah."

"I can't believe that a murderer lives in such a peaceful little town. And I thought I had found the best hideaway. Please take care, Jaden. You probably are making someone suspicious."

That evening Petra went over all the research and the notes. She remembered entering the name Bill Amirkhanian for the 1980 census. Seven Amirkhanians came up. Armenian immigrants fled to America during the First World War. Three Aram Amirkhanians topped the list. Now she was certain their Bill was the artist, Aram. Maybe she should not have told Jaden before being absolutely certain. She would go back to the library early in the morning to research Aram Amirkhanians of the right age, and look up the others on the list, too.

An easy solution would be to ask Bill. Someone tried to blame her for the murder. She felt certain of that.

Which someone? Only Amanda and Bill knew about her.

Her body ached with a tiredness that would not go away. Not since the day when she realized her husband was dangerous, when he attacked her with the knife. In the struggle he fell on the blade. The frustration of trying to get help made her ill until she met McKenzie Anderson.

After all that, she was put on trial for defending herself by those same authorities who were supposed to protect the innocent. The reporters hounded her. Good people did exist as a friend took her in to escape the media hounds. Petra rubbed her tired eyes. All she wanted was to start a new life.

Amanda Perkins gave her that chance.

Petra/Bobbi walked to the library an hour early, planning to do research on the computer.

She crossed the street diagonally from the library to the small parking lot. The first employee to arrive usually put up the chain to preserve one of the most valuable items in the town—three parking spaces that were rotated among employees. Besides the two wooden benches on the corner was the bronze casting of the old man and the old woman on a metal bench. She noticed a third form sleeping next to them.

Mr. Jonah.

Bobbi hesitated, deciding it would be better to look straight at her goal, the chain on the post on the right of the three space lot.

She pulled the chain to the left post. Out of the corner of her eye, she noticed the man's head drooping at a strange angle. Against her better judgment, she moved across the ten foot gap on the uneven large flagstones toward him. Heart booming, she could not help herself from staring at him as she drew closer. His chest did not move.

.   Bobbi groaned.

My staring will not upset him now. A dark stain splashed his dirty gray jacket. An object protruded from the center of his chest. With growing horror she realized it was a black knife handle. The dark stain was blood.

Where is everybody? Why didn't someone else find him? I can't touch him.

I can't.

Her feet would not move until she forced them. Suddenly she found herself running so fast that her sensible shoes stumbled, but she did not fall. Hands trembling, Petra turned the key in the lock of the library, pressed in her alarm code, and picked up the phone to dial 911. She skipped the next normal step which would be to turn on all the circuits for power. Then she ran down the dark stairs to the bathroom and threw up.

When Jaden heard the sirens scream past she opened the door out of curiosity. She was already used to the sirens heading for the beach so she did not think too much about the emergency. People don't realize that the surf can be deadly she told herself as Hal came in.

"Morning, Jaden. How are you?"

"Oh, fine. I've just had a lot of trouble sleeping, for good reason."

"I can imagine. That's been happening to me, too. This time it was my fault."

"Really?"

"Sandy and I went out to a swing dance. Where she gets her energy, I don't know." Hal said with a yawn.

He added, "I admit to having a bit of trouble keeping up with her. I drank two cups of coffee last night."

"Oh, no."

"Right. Wide awake all night. And, I think, so were a couple of dogs in our block by Third and Dolores. Howling. From about four a.m. I tossed and turned all night. Now this morning I've had three cups! Don't know if I can last until noon."

"Would you like the day off?"

"No. I'll manage. Hey, more sirens."

"Someone is in trouble at the beach?"

"Early for anyone to be in the water. Sounds close. Let me see."

Hal disappeared for a few minutes and returned, saying, "It's about two blocks down. People are flocking toward Lincoln and Sixth."

"The library?" Jaden's heart began to thunder. She thought of Bobbi and her research notes. If someone knew who she really was and had been following her…

"Hal, I have to see what's going on!"

"I don't think it's the library. I think it's the little First Murphy Park. Go ahead. I'll take care of the store. No one's here. There's not even anyone eating at the café."

"Thanks, Hal. There are two packages that are ready for UPS pickup from online orders and some sharpening. Those knives to be sharpened belong to the Shell Game."

"I'll take care of the store for awhile until you find out what's happening."

Jaden dashed down the street only to find it blocked off at Sixth and Dolores.

She was confronted by the normally friendly meter maid, "Sorry, Mrs. Steele."

"What happened?"

"Don't know all of the details." The parking officer, Irene, offered, "Not certain what has happened in First Murphy Park."

"Some of our friends work down here," Jaden said anxiously. A sudden cloud of dread engulfed her like a mummy's shroud.

The officer looked at her sympathetically. "Not them. A dead man," she whispered. "He's one of the vagrants. They don't take care of themselves. Don't worry about this one. They don't last."

Jaden's eyes widened with worry. She panicked. It could not be Mr. Jonah! Somehow she knew, or felt, that it was the old man. If it were that poor homeless man, the first person on her list of suspects was certainly innocent.

Jaden walked to her left, to Ocean Avenue, swimming upstream against a sidewalk full of curious Carmelites, shopkeepers, and employees. She turned right at Ocean and walked along the brick patio past the yellow blooming fremontia that she always paused to admire. Four flagstone steps bordered by lush rosemary bushes led down to the lower employee entrance of the closed library. Although she could hear the sounds of people at Lincoln and Sixth, the small white flagstone patio with its stone bench against the wall was deserted.

Her eye caught something curious. The top of a badly stained backpack was showing from the trash can by the door. With her mind whirling she peered at the familiar pack. Something told her to search for a stick to fish out the bag without touching it. If this were Jonah's, it was his most precious possession. The old gray pack stayed with him always. It was his pillow. With the bag swinging from the stick, Jaden knocked on the employee entrance to the basement workroom.

Amanda Perkins opened the door. "Jaden. Come in, quickly." She reached out for Jaden's arm and yanked her inside.

The library director frowned at the sight of the bag swinging on a dried branch.

Jaden explained quickly, "I found this backpack in the garbage."

"No wonder you didn't want to touch that thing. Why do you want it?"

"Do you know what happened, Amanda?"

"Yes. Petra was putting up the parking lot chain when she found a dead man sitting on the bench right next to the Valentine couple."

"Oh, no," Jaden said with a groan as the scene of finding Sergio splashed across her mind so vividly that for a few seconds she relived the terrifying shock.

"She's in a terrible state. After the police come I'm taking her to a doctor."

"Can I help?"

"Of course. Jaden, would you stay with her? I'm calling all the employees to warn them. Bobbi found the man stabbed in the chest, just like," she looked at the floor.

Jaden knew she was going to say Sergio but stopped herself.

"Since Bobbi is involved, I should call her attorney right away."

Amanda stared at her and then nodded. She handed Jaden her cell phone. Jaden called McKenzie Anderson in San Diego. After she explained, she thought they had been cut off because of the silence. McKenzie finally cleared his throat several times.

"What's going on there, Jaden?"

"Just what I said. She was going to work when she found the body of the homeless man."

"And he was stabbed?"

"That's what Petra told Amanda."

"Normally Carmel is a great place for a get-away. This is not believable. I'm going to put off what I can and fly to Monterey tomorrow."

"Thank you, McKenzie."

"And do me a favor."

"What is it?"

"Both of you go to your apartments and stay there. Don't talk to anyone." He hung up.

He probably wanted to say don't find any more bodies. Jaden went to the staff room. Petra/Bobbi was sitting in the one lounge chair, her face tearstained, clutching a full mug of tea.

She gently removed the cup from the woman's hands and placed it into the open microwave. She closed the door and set the keypad to warm beverage. If Bobbi did not want it, she would drink it herself. Though she was not much of a drinker, she could certainly use something stronger right now. She thought that Bobbi, too, could use something stronger than tea.

"Jaden?" Bobbi questioned, as though she had just noticed her presence.

"I'm warming our tea."

Bobbi's golden-flecked hazel eyes sparkled with tears. "He was on the bench. It was like seeing three statues instead of two. He was just as lifeless as the bronze couple."

The microwave beeped. "Was it Mr. Jonah?" Jaden handed her the hot tea.

Bobbi swallowed hard and nodded.

Jaden sighed and sank down to a chair at the old, round, golden oak table.

Staring at the wall, Bobbi began to talk, "The knife handle was sticking out of his chest. Blood. There was blood." Her voice trailed off.

Jaden noticed her heavy, uneven breathing. She found a small lap robe and covered her.

"You don't have to talk right now."

"What am I going to do?" Fresh tears stained the woman's face. "Who is going to believe me? They will never leave me alone!"

"Yes, they will," Jaden insisted, her voice low. "Keep believing that. We are going to find out who the killer is and why he did it."

Bobbi's eyes finally turned toward her.

"Aren't you angry?" Jaden asked. "Someone might be trying to blame you for these killings. If that knife is from our shop, I'm also a target."

"You're right." Bobbi's eyes narrowed. "But how did they know about me?"

"There could be several ways. Several leaks of the information from different sources."

"Oh, Jaden, it's that I've never gotten over the shock of seeing the knife in my husband's chest. Blood everywhere. Realizing he was dead. Trying to explain. Now to see another…."

A flash picture of finding Sergio illuminated Jaden's mind. "We're going to solve this. I swear it," she promised Bobbi.

Bobbi stood up and reached for the paper towel holder. She ran cold water in the sink and wet the towel to wipe her face. "We have to find out what happened. I cannot go through…through another trial. I did not murder my husband. The man tried to kill me and if he hadn't been so drunk that he stumbled, he would have succeeded. Being accused was so unfair!"

"I know," Jaden said in her most soothing tone. "I've found something that might help us." She went into the workroom and picked up the stick to swing the dirty backpack onto the old round oak kitchen table.

She saw recognition in Bobbi's eyes. "Is that the old man's?" The librarian asked.

"You recognize it, too."

"I'm almost certain he didn't have the bag with him on the bench."

"I found it in the garbage right outside the steps coming down to here. This is garbage day. It might have been picked up before anyone noticed. Someone deliberately brought the pack over here to toss it."

"Or go through it."

"I think they might not have had time. Maybe a car came by or for some reason they had to get away quickly. The stick is in case there are fingerprints. How can we search it without leaving fingerprints ourselves? And before the police get hold of it."

Bobbi walked over to one of the kitchen drawers and pulled out a pair of metal tongs. "I don't know why someone left these. The silverware keeps disappearing."

She lifted the main flap of the pack, which, fortunately was not buckled, and pulled out an old, musty smelling brown pullover wool sweater with some moth holes. Bobbi dropped it on the table. "Let's cover the table with newspaper," she said. "This is where we eat. I'll have to wash the table down with disinfectant, anyway."

She went out to the workroom and brought back several old newspapers that they used to cover the table.

Jaden pulled out four mismatched socks of various gray tones. Once they might have been white. Jaden remembered that she could have given him ten pairs of her husband's socks. She swallowed hard. Next was a black T-shirt with Harley Davidson stamped in white letters.

A small wool blanket with a few holes came next. Inside the folds of the blanket were a dark blue knitted cap and scarf. Bobbi pulled out a small plastic bag containing two power bars and some crumbled cookies.

"There's one more little bag. That's all," Bobbi said, pulling out a small, clear bag with a dried-up, motel sized bar of soap, a toothbrush and some toothpaste, and a used to be pink but was now gray plastic disposable razor

"He never used that," Jaden commented.

"Maybe he did at one time. The homeless get discouraged after months of being shunned. He spent a lot of time reading in the library. And, of course, we don't know the state of his mind. Some problem there. He would spend hours scribbling in a notebook."

"Where's that? Bobbi, try the side pocket."

Bobbi pulled out six one dollar bills and some change. Five quarters and about twenty pennies, three dimes, and five nickels. "He probably found change on the street or begged money."

Next came three nicely sharpened but half sized pencils and a white ballpoint pen with "A Slice of Carmel" printed on the side. *So he went into the store.* Did he take a knife? When did that happen? She would have noticed him. Maybe not.

With the tongs Bobbi carefully pulled out a worn, letter sized envelope that contained two pictures. One was the picture of a smiling, round faced baby. Nothing was written on the back of the picture. The other was a picture of a man and a woman and a little girl about four years old.

Again, nothing written on the back except for a date, 4/22/1990. Could have been the same baby.

"Do you think that's him?" Bobbi asked what Jaden was thinking. "Fifteen years ago he might have been a perfectly normal man with a perfectly normal family."

"It could be Jonah. The police would have to publish this picture. Maybe someone could identify him. Maybe his relatives have been searching for him."

"I'm going to make copies." One by one, Bobbi picked up the pictures with the tongs and carried them into the workroom copier. "I don't think these were important if the killer saw them."

"He probably didn't have time," Jaden said, wondering how much time they had left before anyone came downstairs to talk to Bobbi.

After the pictures were replaced in the envelope, Bobbi said, "I can't keep this copy in my desk. I'm sure they will search my things." She pulled down a book of Renoir's art from the valuable art books that were kept on a shelf in the workroom. She carefully placed the copy in the middle and returned it to the shelf.

Returning to the kitchen Bobbi picked up the tongs again. "There's nothing else in here. She poked at the bag. "Wait a minute. There's something harder. Here."

Jaden took the tongs and poked, too. Between the main part of the bag and the outside pocket there was something harder than material. She peered inside. "There's a zipper! Easy to miss."

With Bobbi holding the bag, she managed to unzip the pocket. Inside she grabbed the edge of the notebook and pulled it out.

"How are we going to look at it before someone comes?" Bobbi asked. "We've been down here a long time and someone from the police will come soon."

"I'm sure you're right. This is tampering on a grand scale already. Both of us want to read the notebook. Do you realize there will be a penalty if we keep it?"

Bobbi nodded at the same time she pulled open the bottom kitchen drawer. "Here for now. I don't know what else to do. I understand we can get into trouble, but aren't we already in trouble?"

Jaden had to smile in spite of everything. "It's like being charged with jaywalking when they think you might be a murderer." She put the notebook in the drawer and Bobbi covered it with a small package of napkins.

They put everything back in the pack and with the stick Jaden carried the backpack to where she had left it originally.

The phone ringing right in front of her made her jump. She automatically picked up the receiver and said hello. "Jaden?" Amanda's voice asked. "How is Petra?"

"About a thousand percent better than when you went upstairs."

"Thank God. I've called everyone to warn them. When they come into the library or during the workday, they aren't supposed to say anything about the murder. They don't know anything anyway so they shouldn't be talking. I've kept the phone line busy. The police could not have gotten through if they tried. They may just come over. Then I'll take Petra to the doctor, even if she does seem better. She hasn't gotten over her husband and the trial yet."

After Jaden hung up she asked Bobbi, "Who has access to Amanda's office?"

"Everyone." Bobbi was taking large sips of her once more cold tea. "It's never locked. She believes that employees and patrons should feel free to talk to her any time they want. The open door policy. Luckily, she has the personality for it. I was in charge of my library branch in San Diego and loved hiding in some corner so I could get my work done. After that I didn't mind talking to people. I enjoyed talking to the patrons."

"Who comes into the library, besides the people who check out books and CDs?"

"Let's see. The custodians. They come about four in the morning."

Something about that seemed familiar to Jaden. Whatever the elusive fact was it would nag at her until she remembered.

"And the volunteers," Bobbi added.

"How many volunteers do you have?"

"There are nine. You probably know several of them. They usually come during open hours or hours when we work. None of them has a key or an alarm code."

"So, regular employees, custodians, and volunteers have access to Amanda's office. And the public. Wouldn't someone notice if people walked in there?"

"We're so busy most of the time. I confess, when I'm helping someone I never look at Amanda's door. I can see it if I deliberately look into that corner of the reference room."

"That big picture window in her office can plainly be seen from the street. Someone could easily tell whether or not she was in the room."

Bobbi's voice sounded chilled. "You think the murderer is someone we all know?" She stared at Jaden. "Of course you do. Of course. You're right."

The sound of voices coming down the stairs interrupted them. They looked at each other for a brief second while Bobbi sat down in the one upholstered chair in the small lunch room. Amanda and a policeman entered the kitchen through the workroom area.

Jaden imagined both she and Petra had guilty written across their foreheads.

"They're in here." She opened the door to the kitchen. The police chief and Bill Amirkhanian came into the room.

"Hello, Jaden, Bobbi," he said, his dark eyes sparkling. He stared, unsmiling, at Jaden.

The chief said, "Good morning, ladies."

"I'm going to leave you for a short time because two of our volunteers have arrived and I need to get them started on some shelving," Amanda explained,

"Bobbi's in shock and has an appointment with the doctor at eleven."

Her tone left no doubt that by ten-thirty Bobbi would be on the way to a physician's. Jaden felt relieved that the two men did not protest at all.

"All right," Amanda's voice came from the workroom. "The video, dvd, and cd cart needs shelving. Too bad we just can't close today."

"I'll do that," came a man's voice that Jaden half recognized. Maybe from the police station.

She heard a second man's voice that sounded vaguely familiar. *I'll ask Bobbi or Amanda who they are.*

"Esther, would you shelve the large print books down here?"

"Certainly, Amanda."

Jaden remembered that Esther was a library volunteer. Sydney, too.

"Oh," came Esther's voice. "I almost tripped on that old backpack."

Amanda said, "Let me move it. Sorry. It was right in the way."

Hope Amanda did not touch the pack. The voices faded as the group returned to the main part of the library. She should have left the backpack under a desk

"Bobbi," the chief began gently, "could you tell us what happened?"

"Yes, but it is not much. When I came to work at seven-thirty, I walked across the street to put the chain up on the employee parking lot."

"You always do that?"

"No. The first person who arrives puts up the chain. Many times people park there in spite of the sign. If they see the chain they realize it's closed. Prevents trouble."

"The library doesn't open until eleven. When do you start work?" Bill asked.

Bobbi stared at him, her golden-hazel eyes rimmed with red. "Normally I come at nine, but I needed to catch up on my work. It's easiest when it's quiet."

She sounded normal. Jaden wondered if the policemen thought what was running through her own mind. Who deliberately comes to work an hour and a half early? Jaden knew Bobbi wanted to research the backgrounds of the people they suspected, including one man who stood right next to her. Could he be the artist that she admired? One glance at his thoughtful dark eyes and she knew that they held some secret.

Jaden said, "Would you like to sit down? It might be more relaxed. You know that Bobbi has had a terrible shock."

The chief answered, "Yes, of course," and sank to a chair. Bill took a chair in the corner. That left one empty chair in the room. Jaden imagined that the empty chair represented the person they sought in what was now two murders, probably the only two murders here all year.

"When did you notice the dead man on the bench?" the chief asked.

"First, I thought he was just sleeping. There are three benches and they make a better bed than the ground. His head, though…."

"Yes?" Bill questioned.

"His head seemed to be at a strange angle. I hesitated to go over because staring or talking to the homeless often aggravates them. After fastening the chain I could not keep myself from walking toward him. That's when I saw the knife handle, blood on his jacket. I knew he was dead."

"How could you be certain?"

"I wasn't positive. I *thought* he was dead. I wish someone else had found him."

"He was on the park side of the bronze statue under some overhanging Pride of Madeira bushes. That's why no one noticed," Bill explained. "Did you see anyone?"

"Just the usual. City workers getting off the bus across from the library. Garbage trucks. It was a little early for the tourists. The bronze man's outstretched arms hid him even more from sight. Anyone glancing over would have thought he was just sleeping."

"Did you know the dead man?"

"Everybody knew him. They called him Mr. Jonah. He must have had another name."

"He's been one of the local homeless for six years that I can remember. Once the parking officer saw him going through garbage. She yelled, 'Jonah! Stop that!' He answered, 'Please call me Mr. Jonah.' The name stuck. Can you think of anything else, anything at all? Some little detail that did not seem normal?" the chief asked.

Bobbi closed her eyes. When she opened them she shook her head no.

Jaden interrupted, "I have something. When I came down Ocean to the library...."

"Why are you here, Jaden?" Bill asked directly. "Did you call her, Bobbi?"

"No. I was too upset. It was all I could do to call 911. I spent half an hour being sick. Amanda came in about eight-fifteen and made me sit down with some tea."

Jaden explained, "I heard the sirens. They did not seem to be going to the beach. I got worried about my friends down here."

She caught a glance between Bill and the chief. *It does sound thin,* she thought.

"I'm sorry," the chief said. "What were you going to tell us?"

"Sixth and Dolores was blocked off, so I came down Ocean Avenue to the employee entrance to the library. There was a backpack in the garbage can. It looked so much like the pack that Mr. Jonah carried that I fished it out. Today is garbage collection day. It would normally have been gone by ten a.m." She showed them the bag that Amanda had moved next to the wall by the outside entry door.

"You knew Jonah was dead?" Bill questioned the librarian.

"No. The parking control officer told me one of the vagrants was dead. When I walked down the patio steps, seeing the pack in the garbage can struck me as odd. The bag might have been lost or stolen and someone wanted to get rid of it."

"When did you find out Jonah was murdered?"

"Bobbi told me when I was trying to calm her after I came in."

"You recognize the backpack?"

Bobbi interrupted. "We both agree that it looks like the pack the man used."

"And he never turned loose of it," Jaden offered. "It was always with him."

"You can't be positive, though?" The chief rubbed his chin.

Jaden insisted "I'm ninety-nine per cent sure. Not absolutely positive, but if you did not find his pack with him, this must be it."

"I've seen him with the pack myself and it does look like his," Bill agreed.

"You used that stick to bring it in here?" the chief asked with a quick grin.

"I was afraid of ruining fingerprints, if there were any." Jaden felt guilty now. The two policemen must sense that she was lying. Her guilt must show in her face.

Amanda returned to the kitchen. "Time for the appointment with the doctor, Bobbi. You look absolutely terrible and need some rest. After the doctor I'm taking you home." She handed Bobbi her purse. "Gentlemen."

Both of the policemen nodded.

"My work," Bobbi protested.

"Forget that," Amanda said. "Too much dedication. Take the day off to visit the doctor and get some rest."

"Jaden might bring my folder to me," Bobbi protested. "That would be all right."

"Fine, let's go. We have to get to Monterey in twenty minutes."

"We'll take the pack to examine," the chief said. "You all believe it belonged to the dead man, Mr. Jonah?"

"It was found in the garbage outside the staff door. Take it. It's a filthy old thing," Amanda said as she escorted her friend upstairs. "We will be glad to get rid of it."

If Jaden could have one wish, it would be for a true friend like Amanda.

When one quarter of the Carmel police force left the library with the backpack, Jaden searched Bobbi's desk for the folder without success.

She might have left it upstairs by the alarm. Before Jaden left the kitchen, she opened the bottom drawer and pulled out the notebook with some paper towels. Luckily it was fairly flat. She wrapped two towels carefully around the book and slipped it under her blouse. When she left the workroom, she saw Esther.

"Good morning," she said, "I knew that you volunteered here."

"Yes. Have for seven years. Always loved libraries. This is such a homey, pleasant place to work. Normally, that is."

The clear blue eyes stared at her. "Not when someone has been murdered across the street, though. The staff is really upset. I'm glad I could help today."

"Esther, have you come across a folder? Bobbi wanted me to take the folder that was near the alarm home to her. It wasn't on her desk."

"She must have come in in one big rush. I thought I saw a folder by the alarm. That's right by the Sixth Street door and the check-in area upstairs. I'll show you."

"Who else is volunteering today?" Jaden asked as they walked upstairs. "I thought some voices seemed familiar."

"Sydney Allingham and Vincent Howard. They're members of the library board."

Sydney and Vincent? No wonder she recognized their voices. "How nice of you all to volunteer at the library."

"It's my pleasure. I always believe in giving back to the community," Esther said. "I hate to bore people with stories of my childhood, but when I was a little girl, we actually had neighbors who visited with each other and looked out for each other."

"Not all progress is good, Esther."

"Now that's strange. Where is that folder?" She placed her blue veined hand on the cart under the alarm pad. "I thought I saw it here." She searched the counter and the plastic baskets holding checked in books, ones that were going to other libraries, donated items, and books and tapes that needed mending.

"There's a folder," Esther moved the six feet to the counter. The manila folder was lying on the other side of the telephone. "I thought I saw it on the cart. Sorry."

"She might have dropped them here when she called 911." Jaden picked up the folder and opened it. These were Bobbi's research notes. Could someone have moved them? Even worse, could someone have looked inside the folder?

Esther? Low on her suspect list, but anything is possible. *Sydney? Vincent? Amanda? Any of the employees.* She looked at the work schedule posted on the wall above the phone. By ten a.m. five employees, two reference librarians besides Bobbi and three circulation employees had entered the library. Any of them could have looked at or moved the folder. Hopefully, whoever might have looked might not have realized what the notes meant. Computer printouts that researched names. She hoped Bill had not seen the folder's contents because four of the pages featured Amirkanian family searches.

"This is hers. I'll take it to the apartment, Esther. Amanda says Bobbi is not going to work today. After the doctor's appointment she'll take Bobbi back to the apartments and return here."

"Bobbi needs a total rest," Esther commented as she began to check in returned books on the computer by scanning the bar code. "After everything else she has been through, this is the limit. She looked terrible when Amanda took her out to her car."

Jaden stared into Esther's sky blue eyes. "Did you know who Bobbi was?"

"I knew something was not right with that woman," Esther admitted. "When that lawyer showed up in Dolores Court, I recognized him from the papers. I searched through the online newspaper accounts from last year forward and found the pictures. The shape of her face was the same no matter how hard she tried to look dumpy. She has a very distinctive heart shaped face."

"Esther, you are very observant."

"OSS during World War II."

"You were a spy?" Jaden felt like sitting down. A perfect spy. Who would suspect her?

"Mostly, I read documents and fed information to higher ups. Might be sexist but I believe women often observe things better than men. Women were not often sent out to the field. We were sent into unusual situations or when everyone else was on assignment. Rank discrimination, I say. I could have blended into a population very well."

"You certainly do." Jaden decided Esther did more during the war than she admitted.

"Later on, of course, I was too busy raising our little Eddie," Esther said.

"Esther, have you seen anything else unusual that you haven't mentioned?"

"Just feelings so far," Esther hesitated.

"What do your feelings say about the stabbings?" She imagined people would have ignored Esther as some little old lady who might not be able to even hear very well.

"That the same person did both. That they were premeditated," she whispered.

Jaden whispered back the same warning she had received from Bobbi, "Take care, Esther. Someone we know is guilty. They are hiding themselves very well."

"Sociopath, I'm sure of it. They can act perfectly normal, but they have no conscience. Yes, I will be careful, Jaden. I want to live to be a hundred years old. That would fulfill another one of my ambitions."

Jaden could not help smiling even though she felt afraid for Esther and her highly observant blue eyes that missed little. "I want to live to be thirty-five," she responded as casually as possible.

"I can barely remember when I was thirty-five," Esther put her checked in books into a plastic basket. "Our son kept me busy. Little Eddie." She smiled fondly.

Jaden clutched the folder and gave one pat to her stomach area to double check on the old man's notebook. She also wanted to leave before she saw Sydney or Vincent. "Will any alarms go off if I go out here?"

"No, the alarm's not on now, but if you try to get in during a closed time the alarm will start."

The bright sunlight hit Jaden as she walked onto Sixth Street past a gallery, an Italian ceramic shop, and another California art gallery. She felt so guilty with the concealed notebook that she thought lightning might strike. Why should she worry about that? It had already struck with a vengeance in the early dawn of this morning.

Esther's hidden talents whirled through her mind. The killer was someone they knew.

No matter how much Jaden did not want to believe that, she knew it was true.

Maybe it was her guilt feelings but Jaden felt like someone was watching her. She stepped into the alcove in front of Sergio's closed gallery door to admire the beauty of the painting on her left, Aram's painting of the bluffs overlooking Carmel Bay. At the same time Jaden watched the reflections of the people on the sidewalk behind her. To her right, in the large picture window, was a painting by a French artist of a wood with trees in dark silhouettes. She imagined children playing hide and seek behind those trees. The murderer was playing the same game with them. He, or she, could not stay hidden forever.

"I'm going to catch you, though," Jaden muttered to herself. *Be careful. Be careful. Careful* whirled through her mind as she stepped back into the sidewalk crowd.

The feeling of being watched followed her all the way to the shop.

Hal was sharpening a huge kitchen knife with the steel file as she walked in. "What chef uses that?" she asked as he sliced through a piece of white paper to test the sharpness of the blade.

"Harry Miles down at the Third Street Bistro. He could probably butcher a whole cow with this knife. The man loves big knives. Likes them sharper than sharp."

"I know. He's about three hundred pounds. I'll bet no one slacks off on the job at the Bistro." She put Bobbi's notes in the tray of letters and invoices next to the computer. Checking the invoices came first. At lunch she would read over the notes.

She went over everything that had happened, omitting their tampering with evidence. The notebook felt awkward in her blouse. She asked, "Hal, would you like a break? I'll slip into the bathroom for a minute then you can have lunch."

"Sure. Old Jonah dead. I can't believe it. Sandy won't believe it, either. They couldn't have wanted to rob him. Was it just like Sergio's murder? Deliberate?"

Jaden nodded her head but could not speak. Thinking of finding Sergio made her gag. She stepped into the bathroom, took a deep breath, and slipped the notebook out. Searching for a temporary hiding place, she picked the cabinet under the sink.

When she came out, Hal said, "Jaden, will you be all right?"

She nodded. At one she would put the notebook into her kitchen freezer when Hal returned from lunch time.

"I'm going to run home for lunch. On the way back I'll check the post office box. You call me if you want me sooner. Be back at one. Remember, Enrique's here and Kyle and Sydney. All you have to do is holler."

She wanted to be by herself for a few minutes so she could retrieve Jonah's notebook from the bathroom, and put that and Bobbi's notes into a different envelope or something else to disguise them. She did not even want Sydney to see her with the old man's notebook or the folder.

Sydney had gone up on her list of suspects. One thing she thought was that the murderer must be a man. A man would have the strength. There were plenty of women who had the strength and the knowledge to stab someone, herself included.

As soon as Hal left and there was a break in customers, she brought the notebook from the bathroom and put it inside of Bobbi's folder. Her tote was lying on the floor under the desk. She put the folder in the tote and ran upstairs to the small room that housed a microwave, small refrigerator, a table and three mismatched chairs, plus a lot of old equipment. Most of it should be discarded. She put the bag right by the door so it could be grabbed quickly.

She ran back downstairs and jumped with fright to see a man crouching over a counter. She blinked. It was Enrique and he was cleaning the glass with a bucket of vinegar water and a roll of paper towels. Enrique never wanted to leave a spot so he often leaned close. Jaden suspected that he needed glasses because he did the same thing with the big windows. "Morning, Enrique."

"Morning, misses."

"Our windows and cases always look so beautiful, Enrique. Bonita."

"Gracias, Misses Steele. I don't like spots. The knives look better with no spots, too. Many pretty knives. Cost much."

"Expensive, Enrique. In English, *Expensive.*"

"Ex-pen-sive," he repeated. "This town very ex-pen-sive."

Jaden smiled, "That it is."

"Every Sunday after St. Patrick's Church my family go to the flea market."

"Your family *goes,*" she corrected him.

"My family goes," Enrique copied as he stepped back to check the glass window.

Enrique did not mind her corrections and he was learning English very quickly because he wanted to learn. She knew he planned to go to Monterey Peninsula College next semester. English was not an easy language.

Enrique often admired the knives. She even thought he could have knifed Sergio, but she did not believe he could have murdered Mr. Jonah some time around four this morning. The first buses came loaded with workers from about seven a. m. on. Enrique rode an hour from Salinas to get here. *Four a.m.* That was it! That's when Hal could not sleep and that's when the dogs were howling and that's when Jonah was murdered in the dimness of the small corner park. A tragic end to a sad life.

Bobbi said he looked like he was sleeping. That seemed normal for the homeless man. The bench was better than a gully or a cold sidewalk. The old man did not struggle. Either he was asleep or he knew his killer.

Her stomach knotted. She gulped a deep breath to steady herself. She sensed that the killer was among them, masquerading as a normal person. Who was it? The disturbing reality was that the only person she could exclude was herself. Sergio had husbands and ex-lovers lined up to get their revenge. But why kill that pitiful, homeless old man? That night Jonah was sleeping by the garage entrance. He must have seen someone besides herself on the murder night.

That had to be the answer. He spoke to that person instead of the police, or the killer thought he was dangerous. He must have threatened the murderer in some way.

Enrique's surprise appearance in the store reminded Jaden that she should attach a bell to the door in case she was upstairs or in the bathroom when someone entered. If someone knew where the keys were, he or she easily could take something from the cases.

Hal came back into the store and said, "Jaden, have some lunch and some rest."

She glanced at the clock. Only one p.m. She felt like she had been up all night. She carefully picked up her tote from the top of the stairs and walked across the courtyard to the concrete steps.

I hope Bobbi does not show up now. Once inside her apartment Jaden turned the deadbolt to insure privacy.

Out of curiosity, she spread her own copies of the librarian's notes on the table to compare each set. Even in this serious situation she had to smile when she found two pages devoted to herself and her family that were not in her own copies. Bobbi wanted to know about her background and everyone else's.

Well, except for me and thee, and I'm not too certain about thee. The old saying danced through Jaden's mind. Seeing the two pages practically convinced her that Bobbi Petra Jones Schmidt was innocent. Innocent, completely nuts, or an Academy Award actress. "Her behavior this morning was as genuine as possible. I'm sure of that." She muttered to herself, "Bobbi hates knives. I can understand."

In several ways, though, Bobbi reminded her of an actress. Look at how well she had changed her appearance from an attractive media darling to a dowdy middle-aged woman who would easily be ignored on the street.

Jaden's growling stomach interrupted her concentration. She opened a can of clam chowder, put it in a bowl with some milk, and popped it into the microwave.

In two minutes while Jaden washed her hands and splashed cold water on her face, the microwave beeped its done signal. She pulled out the steaming bowl. Hungrier than she thought,

Jaden dipped the spoon in to savor her first taste of chowder.

Her left hand opened the first page of Jonah's curious notebook.

January 1 of this year showed plainly on the first page. Very lucid.

Next: *New Year. My second decade in half.*

Jaden stared out the window. "Second decade in half. That would be five years. He's struggling with the time frame. Living on the streets could make one lose track of time even if they weren't drinking heavily or taking drugs. Meth blows out so many minds."

Next: *Rain. Cold.*

The following pages contained repeated series of numbers very carefully and precisely printed over and over and over. 1, 2, 3, 4, 5 =0, 1, 2, 3, 4, 5=0. And 5, 4, 3, 2, 1=0 filled two pages.

Senseless repetition? Jaden's heart ached for the waste of this man's life. What happened to him? Drugs? Alcohol? He ended life unloved and alone as a murder victim.

Gibberish, something to pass the time sitting in the library? Or something that held meaning only for that poor old confused man.

To her surprise, the next pages held some nice pencil sketches of the beach area.

The man drew landscapes very well. He might have sold them to tourists if he had the equipment, supplies, and desire. The people were formed rather crudely, mostly in the same form, without faces or hair. He had obviously spent a lot of time at the beach, probably sleeping there. His sketches, including people and children (just smaller figures,) always included the ocean as a background. About every other page he had written 1, 2, 3, 4, 5=0. He was not an ARAM. He was a fairly good sketch artist, though. Better than average. She guessed that he might have had some art training.

The next page made her gasp. It was a precise drawing down to the last detail of one of her throwing knives. The next page was an almost giant hand holding a chef's knife. While those knives can look very much alike, it was the same type of knife that had killed Sergio. "He could have been a graphic artist. These are so exact."

She actually felt a chill. The homeless man must have seen the killer.

The following page was a deep gray of pencil scribbling all over the paper. What had he drawn and then scribbled over? Mr. Jonah, what were you trying to tell us?

A knock at the door startled her. *2:30.* Already? "Just a minute!"

Jaden thrust Jonah's notebook into a plastic bag and threw it in the freezer. She scooped Bobbi's notes into her folder and shoved them under a sofa cushion as she walked to open the door to Amanda Perkins. "Jaden, I didn't know if you were home."

"How is Bobbi?"

"Doing all right. She wanted to see you but I made her go to bed. The doctor gave her a shot that ought to make her sleepy for about eight hours. She keeps muttering your name. I wanted you to know and if you could check on her."

"Certainly, Amanda. I was just going back to the shop, but by four or so I'll see how she's doing." She wondered if guilt showed all over her face. Jaden knew she was someone who could not act very well. Her true feelings showed in her eyes and on her face. She really should work on that, but how?

"Thanks, Jaden."

After Amanda left, Jaden let out a deep sigh of relief. She hated being dishonest with someone who had done so much to help Bobbi.

The open door policy not only applied to the library. It applied to Amanda in her personal life.

Jaden locked the deadbolt on her door and checked it before she walked down the concrete steps and across the courtyard to the shop.

Hal greeted her with, "Jaden, it's been one of those good news, bad news days. If you include the murder, one of our worst days. If you count Sergio's murder, it's been a horrible month. Today our sales are up for the first time in three weeks. Not by much, but the right direction."

You mean my sales, Hal, she thought. I have to make payments to you. If I can't, we are both in trouble. "There have been so many curiosity seekers. Some of them wander in to look and they may buy. The morbid peer into the parking garage as if they are going to see something," she said.

A sick feeling gripped the pit of her stomach when she thought of the garage. She had not been in there since she found Sergio's body.

"I'm going to stay until closing. I'm not going to leave you alone today."

She looked at his concerned face. "Thanks, Hal. I really appreciate you."

Jaden sat down at the computer to work on her bookkeeping, but concentration eluded her. She thought of the people she knew. Here she thought Esther Stennis was a nice, little old lady. Like several of the people she had met, Esther was not quite what she seemed. She had been a spy. The woman was nice looking even now. Sixty-five years ago she must have been a beauty. How much reading had she done and how much fieldwork? The government was missing out. Even now she would make a perfect spy. An innocent little old lady.

Jaden told Hal she would check on Bobbi around four-thirty p.m. She walked upstairs and knocked on the door of the apartment next to her. Bobbi did not answer. She knocked again and waited. Bobbi did not come to the door.

Where is she?

"I'm going to check on her." Jaden unlocked her apartment and went to the small cabinet in the kitchen that contained the duplicate apartment keys. As the manager, she had keys to all the apartments. She gasped when she opened the cabinet door.

The keys were all gone. *Both the keys to the regular locks and the deadbolts.*

Heart thumping, her fingers trembled as she fumbled through the pages of the phone book and called a twenty-four hour locksmith.

Bobbi finally answered the door looking groggy and confused. Jaden felt relieved to see her but her own heart never stopped pounding in her ears. It would not slow down until the locksmith came and re-keyed all the locks.

Who did it? She probably should have asked Hal about the missing keys first. If he had taken them for some reason, he certainly would have mentioned it to her. Instantly Jaden thought that the murderer must have taken them. How long had the keys been missing? She tried to remember when she last looked in the cabinet.

Jaden hung back as McKenzie spoke to the hostess about his reservation for a dinner table for three. "By the window," he reminded her.

He had said he would like to take Bobbi and her out to dinner. From the time they parked at the wharf, Jaden felt nervous. McKenzie would not choose the same restaurant.

Her mind raced back to the beautiful day when she and Sergio walked out on the wharf with hundreds of other tourists. "You'll love the view of the yacht harbor," he promised. It was beautiful, so beautiful that in those two hours she decided to change her life completely and move to the coast. McKenzie did not know this and she was not going to refuse his kind invitation.

"I want to take you both somewhere beautiful and relaxing for a few hours."

How could he know what memories were racing through her mind? Coming with them turned out to be a big mistake. She would have to make the best of it. The women each took the two seats at the huge picture window overlooking the water in the harbor.

"The lights on the berths and the boats are beautiful, McKenzie," Bobbi said.

A kayak glided smoothly into the harbor. The girl in it placed the craft smoothly by one of the berthed yachts and scrambled out onto the pier and into a boat.

A ripple broke the water. The head of a sea lion popped up. The creature dove back down almost immediately. Jaden remembered a family of them playing in the harbor when she and Sergio were here. The memory of Sergio's dancing eyes examining her closely popped into her mind.

McKenzie asked, "Do you mind if I ask how long you've been a widow?"

"Five years." Her voice wavered as it always did when she thought of Brent.

"A long time," he responded, sipping his Sauvignon Blanc and smiling at her over the rim of the wine glass.

Jaden had the Domenico's calamari and clam chowder, two that were now her favorites.

You were a fool, Jaden Steele. In spite of what a rat Sergio was, he did not deserve to be murdered. If she had been his wife, though, that might be a different story. Jaden might have killed him years earlier. She realized for the hundredth time that she came to Carmel for a foolish romantic dream.

"Someone stole all the keys?" McKenzie's question brought her back to this evening. "How did they know about the keys?"

"When I first came, I did not even lock my door half the time. I thought this was the safest place in the world. Now I'm keeping the extra keys in the safe in the office and locking the deadbolt every time I leave. Almost anyone who had been in the apartment could have seen the keys. Hal did not keep the location a secret. The cabinet said _keys_ for everyone to see."

"Still, someone here is dangerous, even deadly. Don't trust anyone and don't make any appointments to meet people by yourselves. Is that clear? Talk to me whenever you have a question, day or night."

Jaden and Bobbi both nodded. "I'm not about to take any more chances."

"I can't help thinking about those keys," Jaden added. "Whoever took them could be a thief, but it's too coincidental. So much worse, it means that the murderer must be someone we all know. That means we are all in danger."

"You're right. I feel like moving you both out to some other spot."

"I do have a car but Bobbi doesn't." Jaden sipped a spoonful of the delicious chowder and watched two sea lions playing in the dark water right in front of them.

"You two must keep on your guard. I've been thinking about a retirement place for myself in this area. Not sure about the fog. San Diego weather is great. I'm going to look at condos here. If I purchased one, you could stay in it or more immediately in a hotel."

Bobbi's jaw went rigid. "I don't want someone to drive me out of my own apartment! Some madman cannot do that to me! Bad enough that he or she has tried to make me look guilty. I want them to worry, not me."

"They are worried. That makes a deranged person even more dangerous."

"I ought to know that," Bobbi answered bitterly. "If that type of person is crossed, they become enraged."

"At least I discovered the keys missing," Jaden said, buttering a slice of hot French bread. "Who knows how long it would have been before I discovered the theft?"

The waiter brought their entrees. McKenzie and Bobbi both ordered the salmon and Jaden her calamari steak. She gulped when she thought of Sergio who would never eat another calamari dinner with someone who was not his wife.

"That salmon looks wonderful." She tried to divert her mind from memories.

"Would you like more drinks?" the waiter asked, setting down their plates.

They all shook their heads no.

"I'd like coffee now," Jaden said.

"Certainly," the waiter answered.

"Are you certain you don't want wine?" McKenzie asked like a good host. "A little white wine with the fish?"

"One drink is enough for me," Bobbi said, "I could not handle wine right now. Thank you very much, though, McKenzie. It's wonderful to get out. I've played hermit long enough for anyone. It's not my nature. You've been wonderful coming up here on such short notice."

"Bobbi, you are one of my most favorite clients. Your prosecution was extremely unfair. That assistant DA was trying to make a name for herself and the District Attorney really did not pay attention to the facts of the case. When you came into the office, I knew you were innocent and I knew you would be acquitted. It's my opinion, like Jaden's, that someone knows who you are and wanted to throw suspicion your way."

"Jaden feels the leak came through the library, McKenzie. I trust Amanda completely, but her office is open to anyone. She might have even left a note or my employment paper with my actual name where someone could see. Or, if the computer were on, someone could check the files that way."

"Everyone has access to that office," Jaden said, "and three people we know volunteer at the library. Esther, Sydney, and Vincent Howard."

"I'm researching all of them right now," Bobbi explained. "I needed to do something."

"Also, someone looked at the folder Bobbi left by the alarm the morning of Jonah's murder. I'm practically certain of it."

"I thought I threw the folder down to press the alarm keys, but Jaden said she found it by the telephone. I could have done that. I was so upset. It's where everyone brings in the books and checks them in, so anybody could have just moved it."

"They would look inside to see who the folder belonged to," McKenzie commented squeezing lemon on his salmon. "Or is it to whom?" he grinned.

Jaden thought, *He's so nice. He must have a hundred women friends.*

Bobbi told her that in San Diego he drove an old restored Jaguar. He had done some of the work himself and loved to talk about cars, especially antique cars.

He brought them to the restaurant in an older model Ford Focus. To Jaden, McKenzie was the sports car type. He came at such short notice that it might have been the only car rental available.

"You both insist on staying in your apartments. Promise me you will be careful. There's a policeman right next to Bobbi who is supposed to be keeping an eye on her. He's one shout away."

"If we can trust him," Bobbi murmured.

McKenzie's forehead wrinkled into a frown. "You're right. Don't trust anyone."

Jaden looked at Bobbi. She had not told him about their tampering with evidence, or the fact that she still had Mr. Jonah's notebook. They could claim that they were simply trying to locate the owner of the pack. She could imagine the lecture they would receive from McKenzie if he learned about the stolen, hidden book. Bobbi thought they should go over it together in case she noticed something Jaden had missed.

Their attention was diverted by three sea lions breaking the dark water to play right under their window. Except for the brief splashing of the sea lions, the gentle ripples, and the lights on the boats, the water, cold, still, and dark, could have been asphalt.

Jaden felt the fog lightly misting her face as they left. McKenzie helped them slip on their jackets. The wharf was still packed with tourists who crowded the restaurants and gift shops as the three of them walked against the tide of people to return to the parking lot.

"It's beautiful here," Bobbi commented. "No wonder tourists visit constantly. Have you seen the Monterey Bay Aquarium?"

Jaden shook her head. "We'll go sometime."

McKenzie was holding his validated parking tag in one hand and fishing for his car key in the other when Bobbi gasped and clutched Jaden's shoulder. She almost fell. Bobbi's hand pointed shakily toward the car.

W-A-T-C-H O-U-T was printed in huge red letters on the windshield of the Ford.

Bobbi buried her head in Jaden's shoulder and moaned, "No!"

Jaden and McKenzie both looked at the other cars. Some vandal might have written on all of the cars. No, none of the others. *It was only this car.*

"Someone is following us!" Jaden told McKenzie. Instead of being intimidated as the killer no doubt planned, she felt anger rising.

McKenzie pulled out his handkerchief to wipe off the letters that had been written with red lipstick. "Don't say anything more," he whispered. "Someone might be watching us."

Under the street light his face grew red.

"Wait until we get into the car." He paused to unlock the door.

She and Bobbi slipped into the back seat.

McKenzie rubbed until the windshield was free of the lettering but smeared.

He climbed into the driver's seat with the blood red handkerchief and tossed it on the floor of the passenger's side. He was muttering to himself as he started the engine.

"Maybe we should have left the lettering for the police to see," Jaden said.

"If all the cars had been vandalized, but they wouldn't come for just one car. For all they know we could have written the message ourselves." He turned right on Del Monte and left on Pacific Avenue. "One thing we know for certain. Someone followed us from Carmel. Someone you must know. Can I put you into a hotel tonight?"

"No," they answered together.

"He or she wants to terrorize us. We can't let them do that," Bobbi insisted.

Jaden added, "They ought to be afraid of us. They are afraid of us. Maybe we know something already. We don't realize its importance."

The one thing Jaden knew was that none of them had written on the car because they were always together in the restaurant.

Besides, there was no point to the writing except to frighten them.

"You must be careful." McKenzie merged the car into the Highway 1 traffic.

He turned off at the Carpenter Street exit to go into Carmel. "That's my hotel," he commented as they drove past the Junipero Street Inn. "They have vacancies. We are dealing with someone who must have committed two murders, someone who may be following us right now." Unexpectedly, he turned left on Fourth instead of right, drove down two blocks, turned left, and then left again.

"Why are you doing this?" Jaden questioned.

"I wanted to see if someone was following us. No headlights followed, but of course the person knows where you both live. Tomorrow morning I'd like to come back and go over all the information that you have. How's nine a.m.? We can meet at your shop if you'd like, Jaden. Are you working tomorrow, Petra? I'm sorry. Bobbi."

"Not until twelve. I have the evening shift."

"How do you get home?"

"I walk."

"No more. I'll pick you up."

Bobbi did not argue.

After parking on Dolores in front of the shop, McKenzie followed them both up to their apartments. He helped them search Bobbi's apartment first, and even tested the windows in the kitchen and bedroom to make certain they were locked. When Bobbi closed her door, he said, "Turn the deadbolt right now!"

The bolt thunked in place. They turned toward Jaden's apartment. McKenzie even used her flashlight to examine the walk-in closet. He tested the bathroom window. It was about one foot in height, entry room for a little person.

"Someone would have to be a monkey to come in there," Jaden commented. "McKenzie, would you like some coffee?"

"Love it," McKenzie answered, trying to lift the bottom of the double hung kitchen window. The lock snapped right open. He turned the slide lock and tried again. Once more the lock popped right open. "This is broken. You have to have that fixed right away."

"I didn't realize. I can't remember if I've ever locked it." Jaden spooned some coffee into the filter of her small pot, wondering if someone had broken the lock.

"Who is your maintenance person?"

"That would be me." She flicked on the switch. Coffee began to sizzle and dribble into the glass carafe.

"This window needs to be safe."

He looked out the window that faced Santa Clara Street and had a view of part of Devendorf Park. "Second story and a sheer wall."

McKenzie sat down at the table. "Jaden, I could stay here tonight."

She looked at him directly, unable to ask the obvious question. Jaden had at least grown up enough in the last six months to know that she did not want a one night stand, no matter how attractive the man. Somehow she sensed that if she said no, he would not be offended.

Any number of women would be attracted to him with his good looks, good personality, and successful law practice.

"No, McKenzie. I'll be all right." She poured him a cup of coffee. As she was bringing it to the table, he touched her hand gently. Jaden swallowed hard. The gentleness in his touch almost made her want to cry.

"Are you certain? Aren't you afraid?" His gray eyes stared directly into hers.

"I am nervous," she admitted, not mentioning that she was more afraid of being alone with him than of the murderer who might turn into a Spiderman to climb up the wall and into her living room or kitchen window. "I'll lock the deadbolt."

"Let's find something to block the kitchen window from being slid open."

Jaden found a cookie sheet that belonged to her grandmother. Since she never made cookies, it stayed with her for the memories. Licking the raw dough in the bowl and from her sugary fingers in Grandma's warm kitchen were treasured moments. And nothing smelled like baking cookies. Bread baking ran a close second. On the days Sydney baked bread for The Mad Hatter's early in the morning, the heavenly smell engulfed Dolores Court.

McKenzie propped the cookie sheet against the bottom of the window and held it in place with a small potted pink geranium.

"There. That will do until you have a handyman install a window lock. Ah, the best thing about coffee is the aroma." He sat back down at the table and sipped from his mug.

Jaden was just pouring herself a cup when the phone rang. The clock read ten-thirty. Who would be calling now?

"Let me answer it," McKenzie said.

She nodded.

"Hello. Yes. She's right here." McKenzie handed her the receiver. "It's Bill."

Jaden began, "Hello, Bill."

"Jaden, I've been trying to call Bobbi since eight. She doesn't answer and her message minder is turned off or not working."

"Bill, I'm sorry. We went out to dinner. She won't answer the phone at night."

Without asking McKenzie, Jaden described the writing they had found on the car when they came out of the restaurant.

Bill's first answer was a small grunt. "You wiped the writing off?"

"Yes, but you can imagine how nervous it made Bobbi and me. Someone is watching us. They know where we live and probably were the ones who stole those keys." She thought of a way to spend the rest of the evening by herself.

"Bill, I'm nervous about McKenzie going to his car alone. Would you…?"

A quick frown crossed McKenzie's face. Then he nodded with a grin.

"I'll be right over," Bill said, and hung up.

Not more than two minutes later he was at her apartment door.

"Tell me what happened again." Bill's dark eyes sparkled with concern.

The three of them sat with coffee mugs at the kitchen table going over the incident. "No one followed us. They don't have to. They obviously know this place."

"You're right," Bill answered, his forehead deeply knotted. His left fingers drummed on the wooden tabletop.

Jaden saw some stains on his fingers that confirmed Bobbi's theory. His normally well-groomed hands were colored with at least three shades of what must be blue paint or tint. It looked like he lacked oxygen.

The last thing she remembered that evening was the two of them walking out and waiting until she turned the deadbolt. In spite of drinking coffee this late, she flopped into her bed and immediately went to sleep.

Early in the morning she began to dream vividly. She saw Sergio's body. The blood from his chest flowed to the windshield of the Ford Focus and formed the words **Watch Out**. Instead of wiping the windshield, McKenzie was wiping Sergio's chest and trying futilely to revive him, "1, 2, 3, 4, 5." A shadowy, hooded figure lurked on the walk in front of the lighted boats in Monterey harbor.

The figure mushroomed in size and flew straight at her like a swirling tornado.

She woke with a strangled shriek.

The deadly serious warnings from McKenzie to not do anything alone forced Jaden and Bobbi together. They reviewed their information over and over until Jaden's head swam. The only thing she could tell Bobbi for certain was that Bill did paint. Though he could have been painting his apartment walls at night, she felt certain that he was the artist, Aram. "He paints at night because he works during the day," she told Bobbi. "Where does he get the energy? He needs more sleep."

Mr. Jonah's notebook continued to puzzle them. They both agreed to keep it secret from

McKenzie. "I feel so guilty. He might give up on us as clients," Jaden said.

The man's photo had appeared in the local papers with no response as far as they knew. "I think Bill would have told us, or at least have told McKenzie." Bobbi suggested, "Let's go down to the beach. That might clear our heads."

Since Jaden's head was beginning to ache, she said, "Good idea."

"There are some papers I have to drop off at the branch. Just take a minute."

They walked two blocks to the local history and children's branch across from the park and diagonally across from the fire station. The sudden blast of the siren from the firehouse across the street made Jaden's heart jump. The engine pulled out and turned left, the shrill siren splitting the air. Cars attempted to move to the side of crowded Sixth Avenue. Jaden saw the sign, Carmel-By-The-Sea Firehouse, over the five engine doors.

"They're going down to the beach," Bobbi's voice rose to be heard over the blare, "probably going to do CPR on someone who got caught in a treacherous current."

"The emergency crew must go down there at least once a day." Jaden did not have to speak quite so loudly because the sound of the siren finally was going away from them toward the beach area. She stared at the firehouse for a few seconds trying to remember something that lurked at the back of her mind. Some scene, some fact that she had noticed and should remember.

They crossed Mission Street. Jaden walked inside the library branch with Bobbi and admired the Edward Weston photographs displayed on the lobby walls while her friend gave the local history librarian some specialized requests from people about the Carmel area.

Part of her mind still swirled. Something should be connecting since she heard the blast of the siren and watched the truck race down the street. The question or the answer stubbornly refused to materialize. What was it?

Probably come to me at three in the morning.

"I'm done," Bobbi returned to the lobby. "You look so serious."

"Something about that siren and the fire engine has been bothering me."

"The siren is unnerving. It happens almost once a day."

They walked back toward the main library and to the beach.

Jaden stared at the engine building again. Bobbi refused to walk past the First Murphy Park at the Sixth and Lincoln corner for good reason. They turned left to join the crowds of tourists walking up and down the sidewalk of the main street, Ocean Avenue. Some people were standing outside reading the menus of various restaurants. Others were staring open mouthed at the pictures of homes in the windows of real estate offices.

The foot traffic became lighter as they neared the beach. The fire engine was still there and a small crowd of the curious milled around the edge of the brilliant white sand. Members of the rescue unit were returning.

"What happened, Michelle?" Bobbi asked a woman who was pushing a baby in a stroller at the same time that the ambulance pulled up to the edge of the sand.

"Oh, Bobbi, hi. Someone got caught in the surf. They saved him and I think they are just bringing him up now. Even the surfers don't realize how dangerous this place can be. The ocean demands respect. I have to get Junior back for his nap. See you at the library."

"Yes," Bobbi answered.

Jaden stared at the beach and the people milling on the sand. *The ocean demands respect.*

"There's something so familiar about this," She muttered, almost to herself.

"You've walked here," Bobbi answered. "Today the emergency makes it different."

Once the rescued man was put into the ambulance, the crowd began to disperse.

A fireman exchanged paperwork with the driver and the ambulance roared away with its siren blasting. The fire crew climbed aboard the truck and drove back silently through the busy town that was always crowded with traffic.

Jaden watched the truck go and then turned toward the beach and the ocean. The sand was so brilliant that she was glad she brought her sunglasses. "I have been here many times with Esther, but something else keeps nagging at me. It's annoying, like trying to remember the name of a song, or a person's name that you should know."

"Or the answer to some reference question that you know but can't find the right documentation. I understand. Since you mentioned it, there is something familiar about this place. Of course I've seen it, too. Not as often as you have. For months I was afraid to take a walk around the block."

Jaden looked at the other woman's classic profile. "It must have been like being in prison," she said with deep sympathy. "I'm so sorry about all of this. Sometimes I feel guilty. Then I have to tell myself that one person is guilty. No one else. One dangerous person that we have to find."

They were walking slowly back to the library. Bobbi would start to work at twelve. They walked past Sergio's gallery, Martelli and Howard, and admired the huge ocean scene in the window painted by Aram.

"There's still some time before my shift. Let's go in and see those paintings again. Some day I will compliment Bill and see what he says."

Vincent, head down, was working a computer at his desk in the back.

"I love this one," Bobbi's hazel eyes sparkled with pleasure as she looked at "Bluff Overlooking Carmel River." She added, "The water seems to change as you look at it."

The artist, Aram, must have set his easel on the bluff and painted the beach and river so that Jaden felt she was there with him. It was like those sidewalk pictures in the P.L. Travers books she had read as a child. You could step right in.

"He's one of our most popular artists now. His values are rising." The voice behind them startled Jaden. She had not heard any footsteps on the old granite floor.

Vincent recognized them only after they both turned. "Ladies," he said with a smile. "You have a wonderful eye for art, like my wife. When are you going to buy one of Aram's paintings?"

"I would buy one today if I could, Vincent. That one with the rocks sloping to the sea is my favorite, I think, although I would not turn down any of them."

"I understand the artist is local," Bobbi said. "Have you met him?"

"No. We deal through his agent. I believe he vacations here for a month every year and lives in Spain. He does three paintings on each of his trips, at least he starts them. The finished paintings are so large that we do the framing. Four years ago you could have purchased one of his paintings for $1200. In fact, one of your tenants, Sydney Allingham, bought one when we first began to sell Aram's work. What a good eye for art he has. That painting would now sell for $16,000. Good eye and willing to invest in art."

"Does Aram do anything smaller?" Jaden thought, *smaller painting, smaller price.*

"Not that I know of. He probably started small, but he seems to like to work in that large size, usually three by five or six feet. They are spectacular and go well in the larger homes in the Pebble Beach area. My wife always says that she loves his work."

Jaden remembered how perfectly the scene of the Lone Cypress fit into Kyle and Sydney's apartment. It made the apartment seem much larger than Jaden's.

"I'm really going to think about it, Vincent," Jaden said. *Maybe I can go without food for two years or so.*

"Thank you, ladies. Drop by any time."

As they were leaving the gallery, Jaden caught the image of someone familiar entering. She turned to look at the woman she was certain was the widowed Marian Martelli.

"It's Marian."

"The gallery is half hers now," Bobbi said. "Hopefully, Sergio's business dealings were secure enough so that she won't have any more financial worries."

"I don't know if I'd like to be in business with her," Jaden speculated. "I'm very lucky Hal is so good-natured."

"It may not be all business," Bobbi answered. "Vincent has begun to escort Marian to a number of events like symphony concerts and parties."

"Really? What about Vincent's wife?"

"He is a widower. That's all I know so far."

"A widower? I got a different...." They walked up the steps to the lobby of the library. Jaden checked out two new books from the lobby display while the librarian went downstairs to get ready for her shift.

When she came back up, Bobbi told Jaden, "Esther did not come in for her volunteer time today. She is as regular as the tide. Could you check on her when you get back, Jaden? At her age so many things could go wrong."

"Of course." Jaden's heart began to drum heavily as she walked quickly up Ocean Avenue and turned left on Dolores. Esther admitted to being eighty-six. Jaden was really fond of the woman but she was ten years older than her own grandparents when they died.

Although the walk back to the court was level, Jaden was breathing hard when she reached the court. She felt the heavy thudding of her heart.

Kyle spotted her before she went in the door of the shop. He wiped his hands on his apron, "Jaden, I need a favor." His face looked pale.

"What's the matter, Kyle?"

"I went to take some garbage down to the dumpster and found Esther's cat dead."

Jaden groaned. "She loves that cat."

"I know. I can't tell her by myself. Sydney and I will get her a new cat or kitten or whatever she wants. The cat is now in a plastic bag. I found a box for a coffin." He sighed, "I put a white rose on it. I can't tell her alone."

The white rose was such a nice gesture that Jaden had to smile. "I'll go with you, Kyle. She'll understand. She must have owned a number of cats. Let me tell Hal."

They walked up together. Kyle said, "She used to talk about her black cat who lived to be nineteen. I don't think this cat was more than three or four years old."

"That is strange. Did he seem sick?"

"No, that seemed to be the healthiest animal. He loved to eat. I kept Esther supplied with scraps so I don't think she had to buy much cat food. The animal must have eaten something poisoned."

Esther did not respond to Kyle's knock.

The drumming in Jaden's chest, which had slowed but never stopped, rose in volume. "When did you last see Esther? I did not see her today."

"Let me see. Yesterday morning, I think. Yes. She had breakfast here yesterday morning. Cantaloupe slices and toast. Let's call her." His was the closest apartment. He pressed her phone number, which he knew by heart. Kyle's memory for names made customers feel so welcome.

Jaden marveled at his memory.

"She is not answering. I don't like this."

"I don't either. Let the phone ring, Kyle, while I get the duplicate keys."

Jaden flew down the stairs, across the court full of people and into the store.

With barely a nod to Hal, who was helping a customer and had someone else waiting, she dashed to the office. Her fingers trembled as she pressed in the combination to the safe. She yanked out the box with the keys and found the two marked number five. In a frantic whisper she explained to Hal, who nodded understanding.

Jaden dashed up the stairs and met Kyle.

"I let the phone ring for five minutes. If she's there, she's not awake."

"Let's open her door." Jaden's hands trembled as she opened the regular lock and then the deadbolt. *Please be all right.*

Jaden's stomach almost heaved when the penetrating stench hit her nostrils.

"Oh, God," cried Kyle, rushing to the kitchen table. Jaden saw Esther's white hair first. She was slumped over the table. Her arms were outstretched and she clutched a small piece of paper in her left hand.

Kyle grabbed the phone from next to Esther's hand to call 911. She must have been trying to call that herself.

Jaden gently lifted Esther's free hand. She was still warm. "She's breathing. It's really shallow and irregular." The awful odor was rising from a matted towel lying next to the old woman's face. She had vomited into the towel. Jaden ran to the kitchen sink for a dishcloth and grabbed the first one she could find. With the wet cloth she wiped Esther's face. At the same time she took the piece of paper from her hand. A pen clattered on the tile floor.

Esther had written P O I S O…. The letter trailed off the way it does if you fall asleep when you are writing.

"They're on the way," Kyle said. "Esther! Esther! Can you hear me?"

To their relief, a slight groan echoed up Esther's throat. Her eyes fluttered.

Poison? That's what Esther was writing when she passed out.

"I'm going to open all the windows. I'm about ready to be sick myself." Kyle began with the living room slider. Fresh air did help. "The kitchen window was already open. She does that because of the cat."

Esther's kitchen window, like four of the apartments, faced the rooftop of the building next door. There was a narrow ledge between the buildings. It would be difficult, but not impossible, for a person to use that ledge to climb into the apartment windows.

"Esther thought she had been poisoned." Jaden showed Kyle the note. "Maybe that's why the cat died. How awful."

"Esther is a smart old gal," Kyle said. "She must have realized and made herself vomit. She never saw the cat. I wonder what made her aware about the poison?"

They were interrupted by the arrival of the paramedics who were having a busy day. A gurney was wheeled in and the first woman to reach Esther immediately checked her blood pressure and breathing.

"She says she was poisoned." Jaden held out the note, which another paramedic took.

"Thank you. Could be almost anything. She looks pretty old. We'll tell them at emergency. Esther. Last name? Do you know which hospital she would want?"

"Esther Stennis. The closest hospital, please," Kyle said. "I'll take responsibility."

"I have to stay with her at the hospital!" Jaden insisted, going to the bedroom to look for Esther's purse. It was hanging on a doorknob in her bedroom. Jaden pulled out the wallet and looked through the cards until she found Esther's

Medicare card and supplemental insurance information that she knew the hospital would want. She felt sick to her stomach from a combination of the odor and her anger. Who would do this? Esther had been in the bathroom and somehow had made her way to the kitchen to try to use the phone.

"Some way the woman realized she had been poisoned. Saved her life," Jaden decided

"I'll take you over and stay with you."

From the bedroom she heard Kyle call.

"Don't touch anything, Kyle!" she warned running back to the kitchen.

"Oh," Kyle looked sheepish. "I didn't think. My hands needed washing."

They turned to find Bill Amirkhanian standing in the open doorway.

His dark eyes scanned the apartment. He rubbed his nose. "That smell! Jaden, do you know what happened?"

Kyle went through the story as they knew it.

"What made her think she was poisoned? I hope she saved her life by making herself vomit. That took a lot of nerve. We'll have to get a team over here to examine the apartment. Tell me what you've touched." Bill pulled out his notebook.

After he made notes, Jaden asked, "Bill, I want to stay with Esther at the hospital. I have to stay with her. I think this is my fault."

Bill's dark eyes flashed. "Stop thinking that way. If someone poisoned her, it is not your fault. It's the fault of the person who is deranged and extremely dangerous. Remember that, Jaden."

The man made her feel as though she were four years old.

"Who in their right mind would poison an old woman?" Kyle asked.

"Bobbi and I have been very careful about where we go and to not go places alone. It never occurred to me that someone else would be in danger, if she actually was deliberately poisoned, that is. Could the murderer do this?" Tears sprang to Jaden's eyes.

Bill's face hardened. "A murderer is a murderer. This one is getting, well, more and more insane. My guess is that if she were deliberately poisoned, someone thought that Esther was a threat, real or imagined."

"I'm going to bring the car out of the garage," Kyle said, adding, "Jaden, wait for me at the entrance and we'll go to the hospital together."

"I'll wait for the police crew and then come over," Bill promised them. "Jaden and Bobbi, you will be careful. To say that something is not right is an understatement."

Jaden answered softly, "We know that. There is a murderer close to us. We must find out who he or she is." She thought, *Before he kills again.*

In the waiting room of the hospital, Jaden attempted to read a magazine. The words blurred in front of her eyes. After what seemed an eternity, a physician came out to talk to them.

"You are waiting to hear about Esther Stennis? She's asleep but doing well."

"Yes!" they said together.

"I believe she will recover. Who is a relative of Mrs. Stennis?"

Jaden could not stop the tears that rolled down her face. "The police have called her son."

"That's great news, Doctor," Kyle stood up.

"Can we see her?" Jaden asked.

"It would be better after we check her into a room. Because of what the paramedic said, we found that she was poisoned. Her stomach was pumped. It left her very weak. Esther's age is a factor. If you'll wait about another half an hour, someone will tell you the number of her room. She'll have to be watched very carefully."

"The police will want to know what you found," Jaden said, blowing her nose.

"Yes. I believe someone has already called here about Esther."

About forty-five minutes later they walked into the room. Esther was lying in bed, pale as the white sheets, wearing an oxygen mask and an IV attached to her arm. In spite of all that, she gave them a weak smile. Her eyes fluttered because she could not open them completely.

"Esther," Jaden placed her hand over the old woman's white, blue veined one. Fresh tears brimmed in Jaden's eyes, and she reached for the Kleenex box that was on Esther's bedside tray.

Kyle said, "Esther, you must get better. Get your strength back."

Esther nodded. Her lips parted slightly.

Kyle turned to Jaden, "I'll have to return to the café. Sydney's alone."

"I understand. I'm going to stay. Would you tell Hal that I want to stay here with her?"

"Of course." Kyle patted Esther's free arm. "I'll be back, dear. We don't want to leave you."

Jaden flopped into the one chair in the room. Her eyelids closed. In a few moments she fell into a deep sleep.

She woke in a groggy fog. Two dark eyes were peering at her through the haze. Two dark, glittering, almost black eyes that she immediately recognized. *Bill.*

He was standing in the hospital room, looking taller than usual because she was sitting down.

"Jaden, I'm sorry I woke you. You look completely exhausted."

"Esther's going to be all right."

"No, she's not," he answered, his voice low.

She bolted out of the chair and moved to the bed. Esther was asleep, breathing quietly. "What do you mean?"

Bill closed the large door. "I mean, for all our sakes, Esther is going to die."

Jaden's mouth fell open. She turned toward him and attempted to block his way to Esther. He was the murderer! All along. Who would suspect a policeman? He was not going to reach her without a fight. She fumbled to press Esther's call button. His firm hand snatched it from her. He put his other hand on her shoulder. When she tried to scream, he suddenly covered her mouth with his powerful hand. She twisted, but her legs were trapped against the bed so she could not kick. She bit his hand.

"Ouch! Hey!" He let go and shook his hand.

"You are not getting to her!"

"What are you...? Oh, no," Bill was still shaking his hand when he realized what she was thinking. "Jaden, I'm sorry. I did not explain. You must have thought I...."

"Why would you hurt that old woman?"

"I didn't. I wouldn't. You can't believe that."

"You said you were going to kill her!"

"I said she needed to die. I meant temporarily."

"Dead is dead, Bill."

He stared at the welt on his hand. "I'll probably have to go to emergency myself. Have you had rabies shots?" He shook his hand.

She could not help laughing. "Run some cold water on it. Then explain yourself."

He opened the door to the bathroom and turned on the faucet. "I meant, temporarily, the best protection for Esther would be to put out a story that she had died. She was poisoned by arsenic, maybe from rat poison. Someone must believe that she knows facts that are dangerous to the murderer. If they believe she's gone, they will not come over here and try to kill her again."

Jaden finally understood and also understood the unique logic. It should keep Esther safe for a while, hopefully until they caught the killer.

"Like a witness protection program?"

"Well, there's no case so far. One of my friends is a nurse at the limited care facility at Bay Senior Manor. Normally, the facility is for residents. As soon as the doctors give me the

O.K., I'm going to have her transferred there under an assumed name."

"I understand. It's the best plan for now until the murder cases are solved. Actually, it's a good idea. How is your hand?"

"I'll carry permanent scars from those beautiful teeth. You are dangerous."

Jaden glanced at him curiously. *Tall, dark, and handsome*. And he probably had the most expressive eyes she had ever seen.

"When you transfer her, I'm going, too."

"You are so stubborn. You are going to have to trust me. I'm a police officer, Jaden."

"At this moment I don't trust anyone." She was stubborn enough not to tell him that for some reason beyond understanding, she trusted him.

She went home in the evening to find a silent group of people at a table in the empty court. Kyle was in tears. Sydney was sitting next to him, solemn faced, but dry-eyed. Hal was acting as the waiter for them. He was pouring three glasses of deep burgundy Cabernet.

"Jaden, how about a glass? You look like you need it." He slid the glass in her direction. She sank down to the cold metal chair, accepting the offer gratefully.

"Bill told us about Esther," Kyle said, wiping his eyes with one of the linen napkins from The Mad Hatter's.

"I can't believe it. She was getting better."

Jaden realized what had happened. Kyle was so upset that her heart went out to him. It took all her remaining energy to not blurt out the truth.

159

"Bill says they are contacting the relatives. Her next of kin lives in D.C."

Interesting, Jaden thought, gulping her wine.

"When we find out about the memorial service or the funeral, we will do the catering," Sydney promised, his pale green eyes misty.

Hal offered, "She had a good, long life. I thought she would live to be a hundred. She still had plenty of energy. This is a bad dream."

"I don't know what to do," Kyle protested.

Jaden gulped the rest of her glass. "There's nothing you can do." Her conscience was making her want to tell them the truth. She hated lying.

"No, I mean, I still have the cat in the box. What can I do with it?"

Even though Jaden felt terrible about the cat, she fought to suppress a smile.

"There's a nice spot in that planter area by the parking garage. We could bury him there. I can carve a nice headstone for him from some hardwood," Hal offered.

"That's a wonderful idea, Hal." Jaden had not realized that he did carving. There were three sets of carving tools in a bottom drawer in the shop. No one ever inquired about carving tools, but now she knew why Hal had purchased them. She ought to try putting one on display and check the website to make certain they were on their inventory list.

She was feeling a little less guilty about keeping quiet about Esther when McKenzie's rented Ford Focus pulled up to the curb in front of the court. The lawyer opened the car door for

Bobbi. Jaden's heart sank to her stomach. Since they were both smiling, she realized that they did not know about Esther.

Bobbi knew something was wrong as soon as she saw them.

McKenzie did not know how unusual it was for them all to be at a table this late and asked, "Do they ticket in the evenings? I won't be long, but I wanted to take Bobbi to dinner nearby…."

"Why are you all here?" Bobbi interrupted.

They stared at her. No one wanted to say anything. Kyle's red face spoke loudly enough.

"Tell me!" Bobbi demanded.

"It's Esther," Sydney finally spoke up.

"What happened to her?" Bobbi's voice was a wavery, choked whisper.

"She's gone," was Jaden's dishonest answer.

Bobbi groaned and McKenzie held her while she sank down to a chair.

"What happened?" McKenzie asked Jaden.

"Esther would not answer the phone or her door, so Kyle and I went in. She was poisoned. They took her to Monterey Hospital and she…she…" Jaden fished for words. She did not want to lie to anyone. "Our Esther went to the hospital." Jaden felt like she was betraying them when she whispered, "She's not there anymore."

Bobbi buried her head in her arms, sobbing.

McKenzie tried to comfort her, "She led a long life, Bobbi." He glanced at Jaden. She turned her eyes away, unable to feel anything but guilt at keeping the secret.

"She left a note," Kyle explained. "She wrote POISON on the note. Well, actually, she did not finish the word but what she meant was obvious."

"Poison?" McKenzie asked, his voice deepening. "Was she poisoned, Jaden?"

Jaden swallowed hard and nodded.

Bobbi fumbled for a tissue in her purse.

Kyle finally handed her a white napkin from the table. He explained, "The doctor said arsenic poisoning. Esther somehow realized what had happened. Maybe it was some memory."

"Oh my God," Bobbi murmured "She did not die a natural death. Someone poisoned an old woman like that?"

McKenzie shook his head and sank down to a chair, his normal self-control dented.

Jaden still could not look straight at him. He would know she was lying or holding something back. She slipped her arm over Bobbi's shoulder.

The woman wiped her eyes again. "We were trying to be so careful for ourselves. We never thought of anyone else being in danger."

"You are all in danger," McKenzie said. "*We* are all in danger. I can't stress enough how this murderer will behave. If Esther's death is related, this person has been successful in killing three people in a short time. Anyone who has any knowledge, or who the murderer believes has any knowledge, is in danger. Do any of you remember or know about anything unusual that happened to Esther in the last few days?"

"She went for a walk every morning, rain or shine. Sometimes she would even walk as far as the Carmel Mission on Rio Road. If she became tired, she would take the bus back. It stops just a block away, right by…." Jaden almost said Sixth and Lincoln but was afraid she would upset Bobbi even more. "Right across from the library."

"Yesterday she was really up," Bobbi said. "She had picked up a package from her son at the post office. She said, 'He often sends me liver paté. One of my favorites.' She was very anxious to go home and try it. Her son called every Sunday. He wanted her to come live there, but she had had enough of Washington, D.C. and loved this part of the coast."

Jaden said, "We should tell Bill. A police team was supposed to go through the apartment. Would her own son send that? I don't think so."

"Anyone could send a package," Hal reminded her. "I should look for the box."

"That's right. Esther never kept things secret." Bobbi's mood changed from teary to questioning. "Everyone at the library knew that her son sent her liver paté that she loved. It came from some deli in D.C. Her poor cat probably licked some of the can."

Bill walked into the court. His usually brilliant dark eyes looked tired, and his normally olive skinned face was as pale as the white flagstones around them.

Jaden knew he was exhausted. His eyes were red-rimmed.

Kyle spoke first, "Bill, can you tell us about any plans for a memorial service?"

Everyone deluged him with questions at the same time until Jaden finally said, "Wait a minute. Bill is exhausted. One at a time!"

Bill gave her a grateful smile.

"All we can tell you is that we contacted her son in Washington. After we hear from him, I can tell you about the plans."

They had better contact him soon, Jaden thought, *before he reads the news in the paper.*

McKenzie said, "I think we'll all have to wait. Bill looks like he could use some sleep and he doesn't know much more than the rest of us."

Bill glanced at him gratefully, but he turned to Jaden. "I will go upstairs. Jaden, could I see you for just one minute?"

She nodded, and followed him upstairs.

"I think we'll be safer if we go into my apartment," Bill dug in his pocket for his keys. He carried two sets, probably a set for work.

Jaden had never gone in. Curiosity nagged at her because the light in the second bedroom was often on until late. A deep wave of disappointment gripped her when she saw the door to that room was closed. *Don't be so curious,* she scolded herself.

Bill sank down to the sofa. "Sit down for a minute, Jaden. Did you see anyone unfamiliar go upstairs sometime during the day?"

She sat in a recliner that was so comfortable her eyes wanted to close.

"I've been trying to figure this out. You must not go near the convalescent hospital. Someone might follow you and find Esther."

"Will she be safe there?"

"Well, I guess so. Esther's son is a general connected with an intelligence agency. It wasn't an hour and a half after I called him that three suits came to the manor hospital wing. One of the suits is a doctor who is taking personal charge, and the other two are types that are used to handling high security situations. To say that Esther is well-connected and now well-protected is putting it mildly. At the moment she is holding her own, except that she is very weak, sleeps a lot, and is not able to talk. Tough gal, though. And a remarkable lady."

"Bill, she received a package supposedly from her son. It would be important to find out if he actually sent that to her."

"I'll call him back as soon as I can," he answered with a deep sigh.

He could not keep his eyes open. "I don't think I can make it to the bed. What a day." He tugged off his shoes and put his feet up on the couch. "Sorry."

"Get some sleep." She stood to leave.

Bill probably did not hear her advice because his eyes were closed and his breathing became deep and regular. She looked around for something to put over him and found an afghan thrown over the other armchair in the room. Jaden covered him quietly. He did not move. His bedroom door was open, but she fought the urge to open the door to the second bedroom. She turned to leave and quickly caught her breath. One of Aram's paintings covered most of the wall facing the fireplace. It was a scene of waves hitting the beach during a storm. Jaden could almost hear the frightening crash of the water.

She stared open-mouthed. The painting possessed the qualities of fright and compelling fascination for her at the same time. Jaden swallowed hard and tiptoed toward the door.

She met Bobbi and McKenzie at the top of the stairs. "You took more than a minute." Bobbi asked, "What did he want?"

McKenzie added, "Was he asking you questions? I should have been there."

"Bill..." she cleared her throat, "just wanted to go over what Kyle and I already told him. He didn't know about the package Esther received, though. And Bill was exhausted. He took all of one minute to fall asleep."

"Be certain to tell him that if he is questioning you, I should be present."

"I haven't been charged with anything."

"You still have a right to be represented by counsel. Don't forget."

"Now, I'm going to see you safely into your apartments myself."

Neither of the women protested.

"I understand the danger even more now," Bobbi said quietly.

"You can still move to a hotel," McKenzie advised. "And I've been looking at apartments and condominiums in the area for myself. Maybe I'll find one with three bedrooms, one for each of us," he said with a quick grin.

To be on the even safer side, Jaden went into her apartment first. "Thank you, McKenzie. She closed the door and turned the deadbolt.

"Goodnight, Jaden," McKenzie's muffled voice came from outside the door.

She heard a brief conversation and then Bobbi's door closed.

First, when she took her shower and slipped into her pajamas, Jaden thought of how she felt when she looked down at Bill's sleeping form, and then seeing the painting of the angry ocean. The apartment smelled of paint.

I hope McKenzie does not find an apartment here. Jaden did not know why she felt that way. What business was it of hers, anyway? She was being about as ridiculous as possible. McKenzie had been nothing but helpful, kind, and protective of his clients. She thought of him at the kitchen table drinking coffee, and knew he was interested in her. Jaden could not help feeling attracted to him. *I'll never repeat that Sergio mistake, ever.*

The bed felt warm and comfortable. Like Bill, she went to sleep immediately.

Jaden thought she had awakened paralyzed, slowly realizing that her eyes were watching a dream scene. She was floundering in the angry ocean waves. Water poured into her lungs and she could not fight against the waves any longer. Someone was swimming to help her. *McKenzie.* He pulled her from the water and began mouth to mouth resuscitation.

Jaden sat straight up in bed, heart pounding.

She was gasping for breath.

The red digital numbers on the clock radio beside her bed read three a.m.

A loud groan of relief escaped from her throat. She was safe in bed, not drowning in those angry waves. Her breathing slowly returned to normal. Her arms clutched for a pillow and she tried to go to sleep again. After tossing and turning until 3:45 she finally gave up. The dream had frightened her to total wakefulness. Why waste any more time? She might as well get up.

Jaden felt for her slippers and put on her robe, pacing the apartment for a while to see if she would be sleepy again. She was not.

The frightening dream haunted her.

"Why waste my time pacing?" She could either clean the apartment, do bookwork at the shop, or go over the notes she and Bobbi had compiled. The apartment was fairly clean. No way would she go to the shop at four in the morning. That left the notes.

They were the only clues to the mystery. Maybe when Esther could talk, she should be able to help. She would not know who sent the package. And if she were able to talk, whoever was with her or the police would hear what she said first. Jaden and Bobbi certainly were not in the official loop. They knew they could be in trouble about the notebook.

The folder came out from under her sofa cushions to the old kitchen table. Jaden took a pen and a pad of paper from her desk and began to re-read their notes for about the fifth time. After about an hour of reading and re-reading, her eyes blurred. Nothing was making sense.

The oven clock read six a.m.

She dragged herself to the sofa, pulled an old crazy quilt of her grandmother's up to her chin. Jaden muttered to herself, "Two of us sleeping on sofas." With a slight twinge of regret, Jaden fell into a thankfully dreamless sleep

When Jaden woke, she looked for the briefest moment for her grandparents.

She did not wake up in her past.

They were gone. She knew that. The next blink of her eyes whisked her back to reality. Her body ached all over. She forced her legs and feet to the carpet, heading for the coffee pot. Some day she would invest in one with a timer that would wake her in the mornings with the delicious aroma of hot coffee.

"I'll offer to work for Hal today," she promised herself, spooning coffee into the filter.

One, two, three, four, and one for the pot. Five. This better revive me.

Grape nuts and milk completed her breakfast. She brushed the notes aside to set her bowl and her steaming mug of coffee down. On one of the scattered pages she noticed, 1, 2, 3, 4, 5 followed by several question marks. She rolled her eyes and blinked, then closed her eyes for a few moments.

"I wonder?" She said aloud.

Did Mr. Jonah witness a CPR scene at the beach? Maybe he watched paramedics. She remembered her own CPR training that, thankfully, she never had to use.

"I'm right. I know I'm right! Should I tell Bobbi? No, I'll wait until we look at the notebook drawings again."

Jaden dressed quickly, grabbed her two sets of keys, locked her own door with one, and dashed down the concrete steps to open the shop.

She almost ran into Kyle, who did not smile his usual smile. Jaden fought the desire to tell him that Esther was still alive. All she said was, "Good morning, Kyle."

"Good morning, Jaden."

"Getting everything set for breakfast?"

"We open at seven a.m." Kyle reminded her. "Actually, we're getting ready to close the restaurant for a few days."

"Close?" *How could they afford to close?*

"It's an organization we belong to in San Jose. Our territory includes three states."

Jaden remembered Hal telling her about Kyle and Sydney's charity relief efforts.

"I know you weren't listening to the news yesterday. There's been heavy flooding along the Colorado in Arizona. Wiped out two towns by the river. We're leaving as soon as possible with our van to give food service for the displaced people."

"Oh, Kyle."

"We have a standing list of supplies that Sydney called into a grocery chain early this morning. All Syd had to do was call and they knew what we wanted. They will be delivered to the warehouse where the van is stored and we'll leave this afternoon."

"You'll drive all night, won't you?"

"Yes."

"Kyle, take care. It's a wonderful thing you and Sydney are doing."

"Thanks, Jaden. We designed the van. Someday we'll show it to you. Before we leave, I'll give you my cell phone number in case you find out more information about the service for Esther. This is a nightmare. I liked her."

She felt glad that Kyle would be away for some time. She hated lying to him.

"Can I do anything?"

"Well, you could. Enrique is going to close for us today, but he'll have cash. Normally, we make a deposit every afternoon. Could you keep that in your safe? We've been thinking about buying one but keep putting it off."

"Of course. You think he can handle the restaurant by himself today?"

"Another chef friend is cooking because it's his day off. They're glad to have the work.

Enrique is smart and responsible. He will close if he runs into any problems."

"I'll check with him every once in a while and see how he's doing."

"Thank you very much, Jaden. What a week this has been."

Kyle ran upstairs while Jaden turned to open the shop. About an hour later she saw the two men leave, each wearing backpacks and each carrying a large cooler.

Hal came in around eleven and she told him what had happened.

"Need to wash up. I searched the dumpster and finally found what I think is the box Esther received in the recycling. Look." Hal pointed. "It has her address only."

"No return address?" She had forgotten Hal's mentioning that he would look for the box. It was a good idea. After trash collection day the box would have been gone forever.

"No, and I imagine it's too late for fingerprints. You see it was mailed plain ground mail. There's no insurance or return request, priority mail, or anything that would lead back to the murderer. You and I mail enough packages to know that no return address is suspicious enough. Then when you realize there have been three murders. This small police force is not equipped to investigate that many homicides. They've had detectives from Monterey help with a forensic team. I'm going to take it to the police station. Bill is already gone."

"That's the best thing to do. Wait a minute, Hal. I know I'm sounding paranoid." She fumbled under the counter for one of their largest bags. "I feel as though someone were watching us, all of us. I don't know how. The box is small enough to go into this bag. The station is three blocks, remember. You don't need to be the next target of that deranged mind. If someone does see you go into the police station, they won't see the box."

Hal nodded. "Sergio, well, that Sergio. You know, Jaden. It's a wonder someone didn't kill him years ago. Killing Mr. Jonah was horrible. Esther had lived here for five years. She was a great old gal. I'm really angry and frustrated. Who is doing this and why?"

He left the shop but was replaced by a slow, steady stream of customers. When she got a break, she locked the door and went to ask how Enrique was doing. He grinned and answered,

"Very good, Misses Steele. Doing good."

"All right, then. I'll have a tuna sandwich."

"With everything?"

"With everything. And iced tea."

Enrique wrote the order down and went to the next table, all smiles and eager to serve.

Nibbling small bites of her sandwich, Jaden smiled at the groups of tourists enjoying their time in the town. She glanced around the court to admire the lavender and white pansies in the planters that lined the flagstone court. How could anything be wrong in this beautiful coastal world?

Everything was wrong. She was so deep in thought that she did not notice the shadow of a person block the sunlight, casting shade on part of the table. She looked up to see Marian Martelli standing beside her.

"Hello, Jaden." She asked, "Are you expecting anyone? I hate to eat alone."

Jaden groaned to herself.

She could not do anything except to smile weakly and nod. "Please sit down."

Marian ordered a cup of coffee and a croissant without even looking at Enrique.

"I've heard the sad news about Esther Stennis. Sergio once told me that she must have been a beauty in her day. I only met her once. How old was she? The obituary hasn't been in the Herald yet."

Jaden was trying to fight down the temptation to make a comment like Mark Twain's, *The reports of my death are greatly exaggerated.* The deception made her uncomfortable. It was for Esther's protection.

Enrique brought Marian's order almost immediately. She glanced up briefly and finally noticed that her waiter was Enrique.

She half-glared at him.

"Where is Kyle? He is always here."

This gave Jaden a welcome excuse to change the subject. "Have you heard of the flooding along the Colorado River?"

Marian nodded, "Two towns were flooded. That's been all over the television."

"Kyle and Sydney belong to a charity project that coordinates with Salvation Army relief efforts. They have a van with a kitchen and large capacity food storage. They're probably on the road right now heading for Arizona. They will provide emergency food service until local facilities are up and running again."

"I never knew any of this." Marian stirred two spoonfuls of sugar into her coffee.

"They don't advertise it. They do it for charity quietly. Kyle told me they used to watch disasters and finally told themselves that 'someone else' could not do everything. They are

178

talented chefs. They designed a concrete way to help that works for them."

Marian whispered, "Surely they did not leave *him* to run the business."

Jaden smiled at Enrique who was walking to each table with the coffee carafe.

"Just for today because of the emergency. Tomorrow the tearoom will be closed until they return from Arizona."

"But they will lose all that income."

"Yes," Jaden answered. She wanted to say that money isn't everything. The comment would have been completely lost on her tablemate. Money meant a lot to Sergio and Marian.

"Of course they say that Sydney is quite well off. From a good family," Marian said in a low, confidential voice that somehow seemed annoyed or jealous.

Jaden remembered that Grandma used to say, *Be careful of those who gossip with you for they will gossip about you.*

Jaden could not believe how quickly she wanted to get rid of Marian. Part of it was guilt. She understood that. She should have realized that Sergio was married.

She could write her own book, *Relationships for Dummies.*

"Sydney bought a marvelous Aram from our gallery when the prices were lower."

"I've seen it. The painting is truly beautiful."

"You have?" Marian's eyebrows went up. "Well, you live upstairs, don't you?"

She made it sound as though Jaden were living in a basement. "Marian, it's been nice to see you but I have to go back to re-open the shop. Don't want to miss out on sales." To be honest she could not get away fast enough.

The woman smiled and stayed to slowly finish the last of her croissant.

An unsaid wall between them was the fact that Jaden had discovered Sergio's body. She could never explain why she went to the parking garage at one in the morning. Marian should have asked about it. She did not.

The small bell on a length of red cord tied to the doorknob rang as she entered the store. Hal had brought it in. "I should have tied one of these to the door years ago."

She decided to put a display of William Henry knives in the window facing the court. The pattern of the blades caught the light, and the handles were of a wide variety of materials. They made an intriguing display that drew people right into the store. Many of the handles were made of ironwood, some inlaid with diamonds or other precious stones, mother of pearl, silver, or desert ironwood inlaid with eighteen karat gold.

Her grandfather's polished bone handles would look so plain next to this display.

She hesitated before putting that $1,500 knife in the window. It would be removed at night. Someday she would have a locked display so the items in it would be safer. Since the Henry line started at $350 the prices put many people off. Still, the knives sold regularly.

A Slice of Carmel was an authorized dealer. They also sold to collectors online.

When Marian left she breathed a sigh of relief. Jaden would never feel comfortable with the woman because of her own guilt about Sergio. And actually, she did not really like Marian. She liked Bobbi. She liked Esther. It would be difficult to think of people she did not like. "The main cause is my own guilt," she mumbled to herself, trying to imagine the killer a betrayed husband. She went to the computer to check online orders.

In not more than half an hour, a tall, white-haired man came in to ask to see the William Henry with the mother of pearl handle. "Beautiful craftsmanship," he said, reaching in his back pocket for his wallet. He drew out a handful of bills. While she was ringing up the sale and shaking her head about the wad of cash, the man asked, "How did a pretty little lady like you get into the knife business? Or are you an employee?"

"This is my shop, although I've only owned it for five months. My grandfather made knives. I grew up helping him. Would you like to see one of his knives? When I found this shop for sale, I thought I was very lucky. Grandpa taught me about cutlery. I like running the shop."

"The papers have said there's a serial killer in this town. Do you feel lucky now?"

Jaden thought for a few seconds. "To be honest I don't know. It is frightening."

A shiver went down Jaden's spine thinking that she might be alone in the shop speaking to the killer. A well-off, very pleasant murderer.

The man moved his fingers through his white hair. "Where is your grandpa's knife? I would like to see it."

Jaden walked with him over to the locked sword display case.

"Looks tiny with all these swords." He read, "Not for sale."

"It would be the last thing I would ever give up. My grandfather and grandmother raised me."

"Isn't that a Confederate sword from the Civil War? It's in beautiful condition."

"Yes," she answered. "You must know swords. These were here when I bought the shop. I've sold one sword since I've been in this cutlery business in Carmel."

"Some day I will come in and buy that sword." He sounded sincere.

"I could hold it for you," she offered. "What is your name? I'm Jaden Steele."

"Edward. Good salesperson. No, if I'm meant to have it, it will be here."

Jaden imagined that he would look perfect wearing a uniform with the sword at his side. She watched him walk out with military carriage to sit at a table outside. Enrique took his order and the man glanced up to their apartments, around the court, and finally took a Pine Cone paper to read.

She also made a mental note to tell Kyle and Sydney that Enrique could certainly manage the restaurant for more than one day. An extended period might be too long because they would run out of supplies. For a few days, though, he ought to be able to manage.

The phone rang. She answered a call from Bobbi. "Jaden, I've found something interesting. Could you go over the notes and Jonah's notebook again with me?"

"Bobbi, have dinner at my place tonight."

"Fine. McKenzie will bring me to the apartment and when he leaves I'll come over with the items I have."

Since Jaden was not prepared for company, she locked the store for a few minutes while she ordered clam chowder and a large salad to go from Enrique. "I'll pick it up before you close, and put it in the refrigerator in the shop. Will you close the café around four?"

Enrique nodded. "I bring you money and food when we close."

Except for her one good sale to the white-haired gentleman, the rest of the afternoon dragged. She finished the online orders, the packing for UPS, cleaned the display cases, answered questions of a few "lookers" who wandered through the store. The whole time she burned with curiosity about what Bobbi had found in her computer searches.

About four thirty Enrique came in with a large envelope, a quart container of soup and a gallon ice cream container of salad. "Five dollars," he told her.

"Five dollars! For all this?"

"Salad I give to me, to you, to the cook. And, Mrs. Steele, we must throw some away because we close restaurant. You pay for the soup. I freeze soup and bread. Can't freeze salad. And Misses Jaden, you know I make tips? Mr. Kyle says we keep tips. My wife be so happy. We make $60 tips. I split with cook. More tips on credit cards. And I bring family salad and some bread."

She nodded, handing him a ten dollar bill.

Enrique dug into the envelope and found five dollars for her. "I must change total."

He borrowed a pen and added to the receipt total. Enrique handed her the envelope. She could total the receipts tomorrow. From experience, she knew the total would be more accurate if she did it right away.

Jaden handed the five dollars to him. "This is a tip for you. Thirty five dollars is going to make your wife even happier today. Believe me."

Enrique's dark eyes sparkled. "Thank you, Misses Jaden. Tomorrow I come and clean up. I do your windows? And the cases?"

She nodded. "And clean inside, too, Enrique. It's been a week. Oh, and can you do the outside of the apartment windows? The last time was before I came here. Had it only been a week since Mr. Jonah's murder? A day since the attempted killing of Esther? The time seemed like an eternity. She wanted to see Esther but knew that Bill was correct. Someone seemed to be watching them. The court was empty now except for two tourists who were obviously window shoppers in front of the gallery window.

"Thank you." Enrique walked over to make certain the door to the café was locked and the alarm set. He returned to hand her the keys, which she slipped into the envelope.

"I...I...so sorry about Misses Esther."

She nodded. "Thank you, Enrique."

After he left she opened the safe to put the envelope in and took out the notebook. In a large shopping bag she placed the chowder, the salad, and the notebook, topped by her blue jacket. She pressed the alarm code. When it said "secure" she closed the door.

The aroma of the chowder carried her upstairs. Once in the kitchen, she rearranged the contents of her refrigerator to find a temporary place for the gallon container filled with enough salad for days. She poured the chowder into a bowl to warm in the microwave because she did not want it to burn. Utensils and two bowls, one for the soup and one for the salad completed her preparations for the simple meal. She listened to her stomach growling.

Jaden heard the screams of the seagulls while changing to her jogging suit. She heard muffled voices outside and knew Bobbi must have come home. She heard the door close. For a few minutes the corridor outside was quiet until there was a knock at the door. Jaden opened it quickly expecting Bobbi. McKenzie's Anderson's tall frame filled the doorway.

He frowned. "Jaden, before you open the door, at least ask who is there."

"Normally I would, but I was expecting someone." She attempted a smile.

"Oh, I'm sorry." He noticed two settings at the table. "I didn't mean to interrupt."

"You're not interrupting. I'm always glad to see you, McKenzie. You have been wonderful through all of these terrible events."

"Thanks. Maybe the two of us could have dinner another night this week."

"I'd like that," Jaden admitted honestly.

"How about tomorrow night?"

"That would be fine."

"I'll come at six-thirty. Would that be all right? I'll come to the door, but be sure to ask me who I am," he said in a serious, definite tone.

He walked back to the open door. "Is there a restaurant you like?" he asked.

"Let's skip the wharf," Jaden said with a weak smile. "You decide."

She watched McKenzie walk down the stairs to the court and closed her door.

The phone rang. Jaden knew the caller would be Bobbi before she spoke.

"Jaden, Bobbi. Has McKenzie left yet?"

"Yes. Come over."

Once Bobbi and her folder were inside, she said, "It's the one thing I forgot. As soon as we reached the top of the stairs McKenzie stared at your door. I knew he wanted to talk to you."

"He's trying to protect us."

"He also likes you, Jaden."

"McKenzie likes both of us. He did seem different when he saw two places set at the table. He asked me to dinner tomorrow night."

Bobbi nodded with a knowing smile.

"I am not going to get involved with anyone right now," Jaden insisted, setting the microwave to warm the soup. She pulled out the container of salad and filled each bowl. Then she opened a bottle of Italian dressing.

"Sergio was enough of a mistake for my lifetime. Never again!"

"He was smooth with women. Practice makes perfect. You weren't a match for his technique."

"I can't make excuses. Should have realized he was married. Still, murdering him was evil." She pulled the container from the fridge. "On the bright side, Enrique gave me more salad than I could eat. I'll give you some to take home. Since the Mad Hatter's is closed until Kyle and Sydney return, the salad would not keep. Enrique ran the café very well. He's reliable and smart. I'll tell Kyle he can be trained for more responsible jobs."

"Their van sounds amazing. Kyle told me it is set up to make large kettles of soup or stews. That way they only need one bowl per person for serving. The fifty cup coffee maker is built right in. The spigot is outside so people can serve themselves. The oven and refrigerator are larger than in most RVs. It also sleeps two people, four in a pinch. Sydney designed it. They've started a fund to buy another one for the Salvation Army."

"It's wonderful what they are doing. Sit down. I have three types of salad dressing and just crackers. My bread supply is gone."

"That sounds perfect. I think their chowder is the best I've ever tasted."

After the dishes were cleared, Jaden poured them each a cup of coffee. "No dessert, either, Bobbi. I do have some chocolates."

"Keep them in the box, please, Jaden. One chocolate is fine, and I understand it's supposed to be good for you, but it's impossible for me to stop at one piece."

She removed the contents of her folder. Jaden recognized some as microfilm reader printouts of pages of the local weekly paper. "I've been looking at everyone's background. I found that Winnie Howard, Vincent's wife, drowned in a tragic accident four years ago at Carmel Beach. That's why he's a widower."

"How devastating." Jaden read the article from the May 1 edition. "They were swimming. Winnie got caught in an undertow and went under. Vincent dragged her out of the water and performed CPR. It was no use. A bystander called the paramedics. Too late. She was dead. The article reads to use caution whenever swimming in the ocean. Paramedics are called to the beach about four times a week. People don't respect the treacherous currents."

The paper printed a picture of the beautiful beach. Thankfully, they did not include any grizzly scenes. "How horrible for Vincent. It may be why he seemed so odd when he spoke about her in the present tense. Did you notice?"

"Yes. And thought it was strange. Gave me the chills after I realized that she was dead. Do you have Jonah's notebook?"

Jaden pulled the notebook from her store bag.

Bobbi opened it to the pages of Jonah's artwork. "This one is Carmel Beach."

"He slept there a lot."

"The next picture is the one that is scribbled over, but I think we can still see some of it." She held the page out so that the light from the kitchen ceiling shone through the paper. The picture was an almost identical scene of the empty beach in their current newspaper.

"There." Bobbi tapped with the eraser end of a pencil on the desk.

Jaden squinted. It was really difficult to study because of the scribbling. The first impressions on the paper were the deepest. She must be looking at two heads in the water. One was partially under water because a hand was over the hair.

Goosebumps chilled Jaden's arms. The frightening realization stabbed into her mind.

Once she had been at a swimming pool with a mother and two small children, maybe five and three years old. Instead of swimming, the five year old boy's entertainment was to press down on his little sister's head until the mother rescued the choking, screaming child. "Now, Johnny," the mother cautioned. "You mustn't hold Cindy's head under water." Johnny smirked and a minute later repeated the process.

Jaden, rarely violence prone, wanted to smack the little monster's bottom.

Mother put down her paperback and repeated her wimpy, *Now Johnny*, until Jaden left the pool. She always wondered if little Cindy lived to the age of four.

"It's hard to see. Looks like someone's head is being held under water."

"Jaden, that's what it looks like to me."

"Someone might have been deliberately drowned? It would not be difficult."

"Yes. Murder disguised as an accident. I think that 1, 2, 3, 4, 5 means someone performing CPR. That makes sense. Not just another of Jonah's senseless ramblings."

Jaden's eyes grew wide. "The beach was empty. This probably meant early morning. Jonah might have been sleeping at the beach and saw the drowning. His mind might have been clearer."

"He was drunk a lot of the time. You know Jonah had two personalities. He may not have realized what happened at the time. He did the drawings, and they are good ones."

"Of course later he could have put it all together and said something to make him a threat to the murderer. Bobbi, I think the same person did all of the murders. If Sergio had not been murdered, Jonah's killing would have just been another dispute between homeless people. The murders are connected in some way."

Bobbi said, "The killer slipped up. He is becoming less and less able to control his paranoia, or whatever mental disease he has. Sociopaths can behave very normally. They do not have a conscience. Any means to an end. If they don't kill, they try to destroy one way or another. It's deliberate."

Jaden wondered if Bobbi were speaking from experience. From what she had read about Bobbi's husband, his behavior was overt, loud, and belligerent. The person they wanted was able to appear completely normal.

How were they going to solve this?

"You think we can find him from his own mistakes? Like poisoning Esther?"

"Yes. That was a mistake. Esther said or did something that signaled to the murderer. He or she thought, 'I must get rid of her.' Simple as it sounds, that's the explanation for the murder of that poor old woman."

Jaden could not look at Bobbi. She kept her tear filled eyes down, staring at the well-drawn pictures in Jonah's notebook. "The murderer is someone we know," she whispered.

The librarian brought out another folder. "There's more information here."

"What else?" Jaden asked, digging into a pocket for a Kleenex to dab her eyes.

"I didn't want to get arrested trying to hack into bank records. I did the next best legal thing."

"You entered private records?" The invasion of privacy made possible by the computer age frightened Jaden. Everyone knew everything about people from their house address and a picture of their neighborhood to their buying habits. From Nebraska she had looked at Dolores Court on her computer screen. Every street seemed to have been captured on the internet. Someone knew if you went to movies, the ballet, football games. Because of credit cards, that all-seeing someone knew who shopped at her store.

"No. These are available to anyone. There was a small fee. I did credit reports on everyone. Jaden, you have good credit."

"Thanks. I hope I still have it next year."

"Kyle and Sydney have good credit. Bill has wonderful credit. Hal has A+ excellent. Vincent Howard has a good report. Esther did not have a credit record."

"What does that mean?" Jaden asked.

"She may have never had a credit card or purchased a house. Nothing to make any kind of a record. It's strange. Not too many deal in cash."

Bobbi showed her another paper. "Look at Marian and Sergio's credit report. They mortgaged their home and were slow on those payments. If they applied for any other loan, they would have been turned down."

"I thought Marian had family money."

"Had is the right word. I believe they ran constantly behind their income and made minimal credit card payments, so they sank deeper into debt each month. I suspect it was Sergio's fault."

Jaden thought she knew what happened to the couple's money. It went for a lifestyle beyond their means. Sergio traveled a lot and dated a lot. He loved those sensual Italian silk suits. She well knew he spared no expense entertaining other women. Marian may have pushed the problem along with her expensive clothes, but she no doubt was ignorant of the family's finances. Her guess was that Marian was not raised with any financial training and left money management to her husband. It was a good example to leave money in trust for someone so there would be something left if they were foolish with money or entered a relationship with an irresponsible party.

Jaden said, "Knowing Sergio, I suspect that he married Marian for her money. Since the money was fast disappearing under his expert talent for spending, and if he found another wealthy woman, he might have left his wife. Marian would never divorce him. Her sister Abby told me that Marian would stick with Sergio no matter what he did."

"She's high on my suspect list." Tears of resentment and anger burned in Jaden's eyes.

"What is the matter?" Bobbi asked

"How could I have ever been such a fool?"

Bobbi put her hand over Jaden's in a comforting gesture. "You were no match for Sergio's expertise. We all do stupid things. I stayed with my husband for five years after learning the hard way how violent he could be. You think it's your fault. Flawed reasoning almost got me killed."

Jaden sniffled. *Bobbi had been through hell.*

The tabloids had her going out with a different man every night. Here she is comforting me because I feel sorry for myself.

"Thanks, Bobbi." She hated to be keeping the secret about Esther from her friend.

Jaden knew she must keep quiet for Esther's sake. Would Bill tell her if Esther were able to talk? She was not certain. It would be confidential police business. Only a relative like Esther's son would be able to get information about her.

Jaden wrapped the notebook in a plastic bag, then in freezer paper, and labeled the package hamburger. Bobbi put her notes away. "It was a very nice dinner, Jaden. Thank you."

"The credit belongs to Enrique and the Mad Hatter's. I can cook, honestly, I can."

"I will cook dinner for us. It has been so long since I've done anything like that," Bobbi said.

"Now, I'm going to see you back safely to your apartment. Can't be too careful right now."

"I'm right next door," Bobbi protested.

"I'll sleep better if I see you go in."

Jaden watched as the librarian unlocked her door. Only after hearing the satisfying click of the deadbolt did she close and turn the bolt on her own door, still feeling uneasy.

Because of the nightmares, she was nervous going to bed, but finally slept fitfully, tossing and turning, waking every two hours. Around three in the morning several of the neighborhood dogs began a chorus of barking. She heard the owners bringing them inside and trying to quiet them.

Finally, everything became silent. Without dreams or nightmares she slept until seven a.m.

In the morning she had a cup of coffee and a piece of wheat toast. She walked down the concrete steps and met Hal at the door to the shop.

"It's so quiet here with no one at the tables for breakfast. I'm going to miss that coffee. Understand the flooding has receded in Arizona. They may be back soon."

"Enrique came in for the keys so he could clean the restaurant kitchen."

"No spots when Mr. Kyle and Mr. Sydney come back," he told them. "Then I do windows and clean here."

"Thanks, Enrique," Hal said. "You are the best worker we've ever had."

Enrique grinned and his dark eyes glowed with pleasure that was contagious.

"I hope he finishes community college and goes on. It's hard for him with a family," Jaden said. "He and his wife have a little boy. And Hal, he was so happy with the tips he got yesterday. You wouldn't have believed it. He ran the restaurant beautifully."

"I'm lucky he came to the shop one day two years ago. Someone who ran a restaurant down on Eighth had written him a check and the bank wouldn't cash it. I called the store to make certain it was good and cashed it for him. He was delighted and asked if we had any work. I looked up at the glass windows and told him to start right there. He's a wonderful worker."

The morning began quietly because of the closed restaurant. People wandered in, looked at the closed sign, and window shopped in the gallery and the store. Some came in to look in the shop and often they would purchase a knife or a kitchen item.

Hal commented, "I think the closed café is helping our business."

"I think you are right. I can't suggest that to Kyle and Sydney, though." She watched Enrique clean the windows with his usual bustling energy. She squinted through the glass. "He doesn't leave a spot. How does he do that?"

"Lots of practice. When he first started I gave him several types of window cleaners. He asked me for vinegar. 'I like vinegar and water the best,' he told me."

"Just like my grandma," Jaden remembered with a smile. Since she had left the house with their ghosts she had so many pleasant memories.

Enrique entered to do the inside of the windows. "I clean shop when you close at lunch?" He asked. "Now I clean apartment windows."

"Be careful," Jaden warned him.

"I not fall," Enrique promised. "Flat. Good walking for me, Misses Jaden Steele."

The entrance to the outside of the apartments was at the side of number six, von Otto's, where a safety gate opened to an overhang rooftop. A flat ledge about three feet wide led around all six of the apartments. It gave access to the windows for cleaning and for repair if necessary. Hal had safety rails installed along the walls for anyone out there to grab if necessary in an emergency.

She cautioned him again, "Be careful. If you slip, let the bucket drop, not you."

Not more than half an hour later she heard yelling from the top of the stairs.

Jaden's heart thumped, "Hal! Enrique fell! Oh, my God! Where is he?"

"No, he's at the top of the stairs. See?"

She saw Enrique waving his arms and almost jumping up and down.

"What's wrong? Jaden, lock the shop!" Hal ran across the court like a young man.

Jaden fumbled with the lock, finally locked the door without setting the alarm and ran up the stairs to join them.

Enrique and Hal ran down the ledge. She watched them as they stopped at what Jaden felt certain was the window to Kyle and Sydney's apartment. What was happening?

"Hal, what is it?"

"Jaden, call the police and then wait at the front door of number five. There's been a break-in or a robbery."

"They were only gone four days!" With shaking hands Jaden unlocked her own apartment door and called the Carmel police. The dispatcher repeated, "Dolores Street Court?" with a voice full of surprise, controlling what must be the desire to say, *NOT AGAIN?*

"Yes, it's Dolores Street Court. An apartment upstairs has been robbed."

"Do you need an ambulance?" she asked.

"No. I don't think so. The apartment was empty as far as I know."

"Then I'll send an officer over right away. They will call us about what type of investigation is needed."

Jaden ran back to the apartment door; which Hal was just opening. He said, "They got in through the window!"

"How? There are window locks."

"Glass cutter. These old single panes are not robbery proof."

Jaden saw two large pieces of glass lying on the rug. "The thieves were prepared."

"They left through the front door. I found it open. At least the glass didn't shatter all over the place," Hal commented. "Neat thief."

Enrique swung himself into the window and shook his head. "New window costs much money." He shook his head.

"I'll call a window company as soon as I talk to the police. We'll get a double paned window. Now, what did they steal?"

It didn't take Jaden long to look around the apartment and find out. Her heart felt like it sank down to her stomach because she knew what Sydney would feel. The frame of the large Aram was empty. She lifted her hand to point to the wall. The cluttered room seemed empty.

"Huh!" Hal said with a grunt. "A thief who is an art lover with expensive tastes. How did they know about the painting?"

The kitchen and buffet drawers were yanked out and contents scattered on the floor. Sofa cushions were thrown on top of the litter. Jaden did not understand why unless the thief thought something was hidden in the sofa.

Bobbi, obviously on her way to work, appeared in the doorway. She was dressed in a figure flattering taupe pantsuit with a mandarin collar set off by a small gold pin in the shape of a rose. In spite of the mess in the room, Jaden smiled at her appearance, which certainly was a startling transformation

"I saw the door open and wondered what was happening...oh, no!" Bobbi began.

"Someone broke in last night by cutting the window," Jaden explained.

"That's one way of getting around the new locks," Bobbi stepped into the room, gaping at the slew of items tossed on the floor. "They stole the gorgeous painting."

"I can't let Kyle and Sydney see this," Jaden said, "but we won't do anything until the police come. I can't produce a new painting for them."

Bobbi leaned over and peered at the floor. She pushed a cushion away with her foot. "I thought I heard a sound last night. Then I decided it was on the street and that's why those dogs were barking. Someone stole that painting and left the sterling silver."

"I heard the dogs, too. Why make this mess?" Jaden and Bobbi stared at each other.

Jaden turned her eyes back to the large, empty frame on the wall. Her heart began to pound loudly. She thought she had guessed the identity of the murderer.

Bill startled them by appearing in the doorway, camera in hand. "When the call came in, I just could not believe it. First Esther, right next to my apartment, now this one next to Esther's." His dark eyes surveyed the room. They narrowed as they came to rest on the large, empty frame. His face reddened. He walked toward the wall, reaching his hand toward the frame.

"They...cut...it out. It's gone." He turned and leaned his back against the wall.

"Wouldn't that ruin the painting?" Bobbi asked. "Why do that?"

"Not necessarily. If they wanted to ruin it they would have slashed the canvas. They wanted to steal the painting. They knew the value." He appeared to suddenly remember that he had a camera in his hand. He took several pictures of the edges of the frame and of the room.

"Hal. Jaden. Do you think the thieves stole anything else?"

"I think they tried to make it look that way," Jaden answered. "Why else would they toss sofa and chair cushions on the floor? And Bobbi pointed out that the sterling is still here, scattered on the floor."

"They tried to disguise the theft of the painting by pulling out drawers and scattering things. Tossing cushions on the floor…unless they thought that there might be money in the sofa," Bobbi commented. "Hard to turn that painting into cash quickly in today's economy."

"But an art collector might have asked for it," Bill said, his face turning an even deeper red. "That's why a lot of private and museum art is stolen. "I'll see if a fax notice can be sent to art galleries right away."

Jaden saw his hands trembling as he brought up the camera to take pictures of the room and the window. She imagined he could barely control his anger, and knew it was his painting that had been stolen. His art that he loved.

"The really hard part is I am going to have to call Kyle and Sydney," Jaden said.

"I can call." Bill took several more photos and then pulled out his cell phone.

"First, we'll get a fingerprint crew to go over the place."

She looked deeply into his dark, troubled eyes and said, "I'll call Kyle and Sydney."

After Bill finished his inspection, Hal asked, "When do you think we can clean up? I need to call a window company as soon as possible."

"Call the company. Ask them to come tomorrow. You can start cleaning up then."

"Bill, early this morning both Jaden and I heard dogs barking."

"I heard them, too," he answered. "It's not unusual for some little thing to set them off. Raccoons prowl the neighborhoods at night looking for food. They can be aggressive. They've been known to attack smaller animals."

"Well, a raccoon did not steal the painting. Someone with a lot of nerve did." Hal surveyed the apartment again. "Was it the same person, Bill? The one who did the killings did the robbery? Too much of a coincidence."

Bill nodded without saying a word.

Jaden thought the same thing and she felt certain that Bobbi did, too. The list of suspects was narrowed down to a handful of people who knew the value of the Aram seascape.

Dolores Court seemed to be the most dangerous spot in Monterey County.

"I'm going to be late for work!" Bobbi glanced down at her watch.

"Let me walk with you down to the library. Hal, is that O.K. with you? Could you run the shop for about half an hour?"

The two women walked down the concrete steps together and walked by the luncheon tables.

"Jaden, how do you think someone carried that painting out? It was at least three feet tall rolled up. You would not want to fold it."

"I don't know. Maybe they wrapped it in a carpet. They meant to steal the painting, though, and I only told one person that Kyle and Sydney were gone. Marian."

They turned to walk down Sixth Avenue, the short block to the library.

"But there were a lot of people who knew, Jaden. Kyle and Sydney had to call a great many people to tell them they were leaving, cancel deliveries. That kind of thing had to be done."

Jaden wavered. *Of course. Bobbi was right.*

A man's voice with a Southern drawl spoke up behind them, "Morning, ladies."

The familiar voice belonged to the Mayor.

"Good morning, Mr. Mayor," Bobbi said, realizing that she had not checked the Rawlings' background. She knew a little about Abby and Marian's family. They came to Monterey in the 1920s. How many people were living here then?

"Please call me Ted. I heard you had some trouble again last night. A robbery. The police chief called me because he knows I want to be on top of anything that's happening in Carmel. Don't want any reporter to surprise me. I'd sure like to find out what's going on around here. We haven't had a murder in this town for five years and suddenly we have three since you've bought the cutlery shop."

Jaden paused in mid-stride, "Mister Mayor, I had nothing to do with the murders!" She felt her face grow hot with anger and guilt at the same time. If she had met Sergio at the right time that night, maybe he would not have been killed, or possibly, she would have been murdered, too.

"I apologize, Jaden. To both of you two beautiful ladies. Our city is graced."

A true politician.

"You knew who I was before I came, didn't you?" Bobbi questioned.

"Yes. I want you to know that I thought you never should have been put on trial. Somebody did not like you, or had another motive."

"Do you think anyone else knew that Bobbi was Roberta Schmidt?" The question occurred to Jaden and she blurted it out.

Mayor Rawling's face reddened under the dark circles under his brown eyes. He cleared his throat. In his politician's way he was trying to conceive a circular answer to the direct question.

"Mayor?" Bobbi asked.

"I had to get some opinions so I asked Constance and the city manager, Barton."

He might as well have published it in the paper, Jaden thought about the open house. Constance Rawlings had, to put it mildly, an uncharitable side to her character.

They stopped in front of the library door.

The mayor cleared his throat, "I'll be leaving you here. Is there anyone else in the building?"

"Not yet," Bobbi answered with a frosty crispness as she opened the door. The alarm beeped. She punched in her code. The digital read of the keypad switched to, "Ready to arm."

"I think I'm coming in to check the building with you. There are three levels. Separate rooms everywhere. Lots of hiding spots."

Ted followed them down five steps to the circuit box where Bobbi turned on the lights. They walked down the full flight of steps to the basement and the workroom. Bobbi unlocked the door to the workroom and said, "Thank you. You can go out the downstairs door to the patio. It's a little closer to city hall."

Jaden made herself say thank you to the mayor of Carmel-By-The-Sea.

"The number of people who knew about me is probably endless," Bobbi said, swallowing hard. "I thought I started a new life. What a joke. That trial is going to follow me forever!"

"You can't believe that way, Bobbi. Both of us are going to change our lives. I do think Constance would tell people just out of gossipy meanness. I certainly could not tell that to the mayor." Jaden heard someone walking down the stairs. "He probably knows how she is anyway."

"I'll go back now. Have to call Kyle and Sydney and I'm going to hate that."

She put her hand on the bar of the patio door.

By the time Bobbi had put away her purse and jacket, Amanda Perkins and another employee had come into the small kitchen.

"Jaden, how are you doing?" the library director asked.

Amanda took a plastic container and a bottle of ranch salad dressing from the refrigerator and set it on the table. She started the electric teapot.

Bobbi stood with Jaden outside the exit door.

"I'll let you know anything new that I find out tonight," She whispered.

To avoid interruptions, Jaden called from her apartment while Hal was running the shop downstairs. She heard Kyle answer the phone. "Kyle." She swallowed hard. "It's Jaden, Jaden Steele." How many Jadens could he know?

"Jaden? *Jaden?* What's wrong?" Obviously there would be no other reason for her to call.

Her first words barely croaked out. "Kyle, there's been a robbery."

"Did someone break into the restaurant?"

"No. It was your apartment. They used a glass cutter on the living room window."

A groan echoed through the phone line.

"What did they take?"

"It seems to be just one item, but it's a big loss. Kyle, they took the Aram seascape. Nothing else seems to be gone, unless you kept money in the apartment."

"No. We don't keep any cash. The painting. Sydney loves that painting. But it's gigantic. That would not go out the window."

"They must have left by the front door. They didn't take it in the frame. The thief cut the canvas out of the frame."

"Oh, no! Sydney is going to be very miserable! How dare they?"

"Could Sydney give me any information? The police are trying to find fingerprints now, but when they are done Enrique and I would like to straighten things up before you see the apartment. Maybe they were looking for money. They dumped contents of drawers on the floor. Your silver seems to still be there. How about jewelry?"

"I usually wear what I have, Jaden, and Sydney does not like jewelry."

"Could you put Sydney on the phone? Do you have a picture of the painting? Bill would like a picture of it framed and the value."

"Just a minute. I'll get him. We're both right here in the kitchen."

"Jaden," Sydney's anxious voice came on the phone. "Tell me they did not ruin the Lone Cypress! I adore that painting!"

"No, Sydney. Bill doesn't think so. They cut it out of the frame. They obviously wanted the painting to resell."

"It's insured for its current retail value, Jaden. It's gone up so much since I paid the $2,000 for it. The company has a picture, so does the gallery because Sergio gave me a statement of its current value for the insurance, and I have one with the insurance papers in my safe deposit box. But I'm ready to cry. It's impossible to replace."

"I know, Sydney. I dreaded making this call, but knew you should find out before you and Kyle came back. And the police would like a photo of the painting."

"If they want it right away you'll have to get it from Vincent at the gallery."

"I am so sorry about this. If it's insured you can purchase another one."

"Won't be the same," Sydney muttered. His voice regained some strength. "Thank you, Jaden. I realize how hard it must have been to call. We should be home in about four days. Things are slowly coming back to normal here. People who can get back to their homes are returning. The power is back on in most areas. The estimate is two days for everyone to have power. Then we'll start back. That will take two more days."

"I'm sorry, Sydney."

Sydney said with a deep sigh, "Thank you for making this call, Jaden. What terrible events. We never should have told anyone we were leaving."

"Once the café closed, everyone knew you were away, Sydney." She suddenly remembered.

"Enrique did a wonderful job of running the restaurant. He could have done a few more days until your supplies ran out. I don't know about his ability to order supplies. He's smart and is going to classes at the community college."

"That's good to know if it comes up again. He is one of the best workers I've ever seen. Jaden, thank you for calling."

"Maybe the painting will be recovered," she offered, doubting her own words.

"Possibly. Kyle wants to say something. I'll be there as soon as possible, Jaden."

Kyle's voice returned to the line. "Jaden, I'd have rather they had stolen the silver, and that belonged to my grandparents. How did they know about the painting?"

"I told Sydney it might be recovered."

His tone sounded cynical, "Might." He asked, "Is there a service for Esther?"

Jaden had totally forgotten about Esther's supposed death. "Oh, oh," Her mind raced for something to say. Naturally something would have been set by now. "Her son…her son…said she did not want a service."

"Hum," Kyle answered.

"But you can make a donation, to," she thought of their van and said, "to the Salvation Army." She knew Kyle would like that.

"We'll do it when we return," Kyle answered. "Jaden, we'll see you soon."

Jaden hung up the phone, feeling overwhelmingly guilty about the lie, and slightly relieved. Lying about Esther's death made her stomach churn, but she knew it was for the woman's protection. If only the robbery had not happened in the first place. *I have to give Hal a break at the shop.* Jaden locked her door, and walked downstairs. She tried to think of a way to make the windows to the outside roof safe until they could be replaced with more secure double panes. She wondered about the expense.

Hal normally went home in the middle of the afternoon. "Lunchtime, Hal," she said when she came into the quiet shop.

"Jaden, do you realize you are frowning? It's not like you. Usually you smile a lot."

"You would frown, too, if you had to call someone and tell them their prize possession had been stolen."

"You talked to Kyle and Sydney?"

She nodded. "After you have your lunch I'm supposed to get some information from the Martelli and Howard Gallery about the painting. The police want a picture so it can be faxed and put out on the internet to art galleries."

"If that ever turns up, it will be a miracle. I brought my lunch. I'll just sit out in the sunshine and eat. Business has been next to zero except for the online orders. I thought the restaurant being closed would bring people into the shop. Word is out tourists aren't even coming into the court. If you want to go down to the gallery any time, go ahead. I'll sit outside. I can see if anyone comes to browse the shop."

After Jaden reviewed the internet orders and cleared up a little correspondence, she called the gallery about the information on the Lone Cypress painting. Marian Martelli answered. "Martelli and Howard Gallery."

Jaden wished she could have spoken to Vincent because Marian Martelli had jumped high on her list of murder suspects. "Marian. This is Jaden Steele."

"Hello. What may I do for you?" She did not sound like she wanted to do anything for Jaden, though it could be her imagination going off on a guilty tangent.

"Is Vincent there?"

"No. I'm in charge of the gallery right now. I'll help you." There was an obvious bitter tone to her crisp words.

She knew about me. Jaden swallowed hard.

"Marian, there has been a robbery here at the apartments. Actually Kyle and Sydney's."

"What? Something else happened at your apartments? You ought to think about moving."

"Yes. The beautiful Aram that Kyle and Sydney owned was stolen last night."

"How terrible!"

"I've spoken to Sydney. He says the gallery has a picture of the painting, and did an appraisal of its value for his insurance company. Can you give that to me for the police, or send it right over to the police station?"

"Of course. It's just that I would have no idea where that information is kept and I should find out for myself. Vincent is at our storage area in Monterey right now to take out two paintings to be framed for display in the gallery."

"Could you have him call me as soon as he gets back? The information is really needed."

"I'll call him on his cell phone. This is terrible news. I realize it's important to have the description to send out to dealers right away."

"Thanks, Marian." Jaden hung up. A deep stab of guilt hit her right in the chest.

If she had never met Sergio, had never come to Carmel, would anyone have been murdered? She realized she was falling into the same trap as Petra Jones-Schmidt. Jaden felt convinced that someone with knowledge of the librarian's past committed the murders hoping that Bobbi would be the logical suspect.

The ringing phone jangled her back to reality.

Vincent said, "Hello, Jaden. Marian told me what happened. When I get back to Carmel I'll look up the information for you. You say the canvas was cut? Destroyed? Not vandals?"

"It's gone, Vincent. It was cut at the edge of the frame. Is it ruined?"

"That depends. If they folded it there might be some damage. The thieves wouldn't have done that if they meant to resell."

"I know Sydney would offer a reward. He loved that painting. I hated to call and tell him. He asked me to call you about the information for the insurance claim if the painting is not recovered."

"When I go back, I'll have everything ready."

"Thanks very much. It's been a terrible week. Kyle and Sydney think they will be home in about four days. Sydney is calling the insurance company now to find out what is needed. Luckily it's insured for the full current value. I'm glad he did that."

"I'll have everything ready and will arrange to bring it over to you. Goodbye."

Jaden had no sooner hung up than she saw a familiar figure talking to Hal outside. McKenzie sat down at a chair next to Hal, who probably told him about the theft. Not many people knew about the contents of the chef's apartment. An uneasy feeling gnawed at Jaden.

She saw him get up and come into the shop. Jaden wondered if she were ever going to get any work done.

McKenzie entered with a serious expression in his gray eyes.

"Jaden, I really don't think it's safe for you or Bobbi to stay here. Hal tells me that someone cut the glass with a cutter and pushed the window in."

"Hal's ordering new double panes for all the windows facing that side," Jaden said. "We're trying to figure out something in the meantime." She did not sound very convincing to herself, let alone anyone else. "I know that there is a murderer loose. And he's here."

"You could move into a motel."

"I don't think we would be any safer in a motel room. Maybe less."

"The robbery at Kyle and Sydney's put real gloom on my good news."

Jaden looked at him, wondering what he could mean. "Your news?"

"Yes, I put an offer in on a condo in Monterey. I'm waiting to see what happens. They will probably counter offer. The real estate market is so dead that they might accept. I don't believe that they have had any offers."

"Where is it in Monterey?" Jaden felt surprised that he actually was serious about buying something in this area. He obviously could afford it.

"Skyline Forest. I could take you by there tonight when we go out to dinner."

Jaden groaned to herself. She had forgotten his dinner invitation completely.

"What type of food do you like?" he asked.

"Oh, anything." She heard her stomach growling and remembered that she had not eaten lunch and the breakfast toast on the run would not hold her all day.

He laughed. He looked like a young boy when he laughed. At the same time she knew he was a highly intelligent, successful attorney. Bobbi's case had made him famous, or both of them notorious, depending on how one looked at six months of being in the media spotlight.

"Mexican? Chinese? Have you eaten Middle Eastern food?"

"No," she answered. "Kearny didn't have many ethnic restaurants that I remember. Usually at seminars on the road our meals were provided."

"There's one I like in Pacific Grove. Then I can take you by the condominium complex. It's a beautiful spot right in a forest. My townhouse in San Diego is in the middle of downtown. This is really a different world."

He did not mention inviting Bobbi. Jaden wished he had. The thieves stole her enthusiasm about the evening.

"I'll pick you up at six-thirty. Bobbi gets off at six and I want to make certain she is safe in her apartment, although I don't know how safe that is now." His forehead wrinkled into a frown.

At six-thirty that evening he knocked on the door. Jaden was ready to go.

He drove onto Highway One briefly and turned off at the Pacific Grove exit, turning right on Forest Avenue. Memories of Sergio flooded back when McKenzie drove past the main entrance of Asilomar to reach Lighthouse.

Once inside the small restaurant the waitress set a hot dish with the appetizer, a small pizza covered with what looked like grass. Jaden wished it had a regular pizza topping.

"It's their signature appetizer dish. Za-tar." McKenzie lifted a small wedge to her plate.

"Try some."

Jaden hesitated, taking another sip of the dry white wine. *If one were hungry enough, one would probably eat grass. Grass soup. Well, what was onion soup?*

McKenzie took a bite of his. "Delicious. It's a blend of spices called Za-tar and sesame seeds. The pizza crust is flat Greek bread with plenty of olive oil." He polished off his piece and took another one.

The Za-tar did smell good, so Jaden took a bite. In spite of the different texture and taste, it was delicious.

"Ummm," she commented. "McKenzie, you're right. I like the taste."

He grinned. That little boy grin was too appealing. Jaden looked at her plate to avoid looking at him. She cleaned her small plate.

The combination plates that McKenzie ordered for them arrived. She asked him to order because she was not familiar with the dishes. She tried what looked like a fried round golf ball.

She cut it and lifted a small piece to her mouth. It was delicious, too.

The waitress brought a basket of warm, flat pita bread to the table.

McKenzie tore off a piece of the bread. "You can use this to dip in the humus. It's ground garbanzo beans. I know that might not sound good, but try it."

Jaden imitated him, using the bread to dip. "How could they make that taste so good?" Maybe it was her second glass of chardonnay that was making everything taste delicious, or maybe she had been really hungry.

They finished with a Turkish coffee that Jaden could chew.

"That was a wonderful meal, McKenzie. Thank you," she said as he helped with her jacket.

They walked into what was a clear, mild night for the coast. A full moon reflected on the water of the bay two blocks down.

"Would you like to walk along the promenade by the water?" McKenzie asked.

Jaden hesitated. Few nights would be as beautiful as this. "Why not?"

She heard a noise by the side of Za'tars and saw the figure of an old woman standing over one of the garbage cans. She put something from the garbage into her full shopping cart. Jaden swallowed hard, listening to the woman's constant inaudible mumbling.

McKenzie took Jaden's arm and they started across the street.

The woman pulled out a rag from the pocket of her filthy, baggy brown pants and wiped her face until her dark makeup came off. She watched Jaden and McKenzie slowly walk down the first sloping block to the ocean before she pulled her two shopping bags from the cart and headed quickly to a parked car. The interior lights went on briefly. The man in the car started the engine. The headlights lit the sidewalk as she put on her seat belt. "How did I do, General?"

"Wonderful. It's amazing. You did so well for someone with no formal training."

He started the car slowly and turned left at the next intersection to drive toward the beach. If

Jaden and McKenzie took the normal walk to the park at Lover's Point, Edward could park at the lot overlooking the beach and be able to watch them. If anyone were following they could see.

"I don't believe either one of them recognized me. Do you suspect Jaden?"

"No," the general answered. "I've tried to study what has happened so far. I think Jaden, and you, are in great danger. Someone knows who you are, where you live. Do you realize that?"

The woman in the dirty clothes swallowed hard and sank down in the car seat.

Jaden savored the sight of the peaceful, clear night with that enormous full moon reflected in the ocean waters. "That's Santa Cruz on the other side of the bay. I haven't been there yet. Only seen the lights across the water."

"It's unusually clear tonight," McKenzie commented. "The moon should be blue instead of bright orange because this sight is like the old saying, once in a blue moon."

They strolled with others into the small park at Lovers Point. Waves lapped on the rocks below. Cypress trees sculptured by the wind took on spiky, contorted shapes in the darkening night. Barking from the rocks of the point meant the sea lions were still awake.

A young boy with a man was jumping up and down, pointing "Look, daddy, look! The sea otters are playing!"

"How wonderful to look at things the way children see them. Everything is new." Jaden clutched her jacket to occupy her hands although the night was mild. She did not want to hold McKenzie's hand because she did not want to encourage him. Maybe it was too late for that. Going out with him was encouragement enough. He was easy to talk to and attractive. Still, her feelings about him were so mixed.

"This is beautiful," Jaden whispered. "You would not know that there was anything wrong in the whole world." She swallowed hard, remembering the old woman going through the garbage. Jaden thought of sad Jonah living his last days on the streets.

"You are beautiful," McKenzie responded. "The moonlight is sparkling in your eyes. They look dark now. In the day they are the most beautiful shade, almost violet." He gently pulled her close and kissed her. She melted into his arms for a long, lingering kiss. Jaden finally stepped back. She was embarrassed about feeling so comfortable in his arms.

He looked down at her, smiling. "Jaden," he began quietly. "I know you've been through a lot in a short time. You changed your whole life to move here and start over."

He had the grace not to mention her original motive, which he very well knew.

"Then the murders. There's no way I want to push you. I like you very much."

"I like you, too, McKenzie. This is such a bad time. Something in the back of my mind tells me that Sergio's murder happened because I moved to Carmel. He fooled me completely."

"The killer took advantage of the situation. I'm certain of that." He held her hand in his as they walked by the Old Bath House Restaurant. "Bobbi may have been the trigger. She was set up to look guilty. I'm almost positive, or to throw suspicion the wrong way. Bobbi is not a killer."

They crossed the street and began the uphill walk to Lighthouse Avenue and McKenzie's car.

Behind them, in the small parking lot on the point by the restaurant, a car slowly backed out into the street. General Stennis drove around the block to avoid suspicion. He would end up on Lighthouse Avenue in front of the restaurant. That way they could make certain the couple got safely into their car. Someone very dangerous could be walking these same streets.

Oblivious of anything unusual, McKenzie and Jaden walked slowly up the hill to the rental car. Jaden's emotions stirred within her. The lesson she learned from Sergio was to never allow herself to become immediately involved with anyone she hardly knew. At least this attractive man walking with her was unattached. Bobbi told her that. *Of course women are after him all the time. He has everything and is a very sharp attorney. Even in the superbly tailored courtroom suit he gives a naïve, childish impression. Others mistake it and underestimate him. He's a shrewd attorney whose mind is always working.*

Jaden had to agree. Even though he was quiet now she felt that he was thinking rapidly.

She was afraid to try to read his mind. Actually, it was not necessary as he had plainly stated his feelings. He was interested in her.

McKenzie clicked the remote button on the keychain and the car doors unlocked.

He held the door for her and then came around to the driver's side with a frown on his face. "I could swear I saw the same blue Toyota parked ahead of us when we went down to the beach. Now it's parked across the street."

"There are a lot of Toyotas," Jaden responded, staring at the car. "I think two people are in the car, but it's hard to tell in the dark."

"Yes, people don't normally sit in a dark car, either. Let's see if they follow us."

He started the engine and pulled out.

"They haven't moved, McKenzie."

They watched for the car the whole time they were on Lighthouse Avenue, but it did not follow them. McKenzie turned onto Pacific Avenue in Monterey to drive over to Highway One and the short distance to Carmel.

"I guess I'm too suspicious," McKenzie said.

"I don't think that under the circumstances we can be too suspicious," Jaden said with a deep sigh, settling back in the car seat. She felt exhausted and hoped she would not fall asleep before they arrived at Dolores Street Court. Her eyes refused to stay open. If only that beautiful painting had not been stolen. Seeing that empty frame...suddenly her eyes popped open.

"Oh! What is it?" The words jumped out of her mouth before she could stop them.

"Is something the matter, Jaden?" McKenzie took the Carpenter Street exit from the highway to enter Carmel from the back way.

"I'm trying to remember," she answered. Her forehead started to throb with the beginning of a headache. "About the theft of the painting. Almost had the answer but the thought is just out of my reach."

"Something important?"

"I believe so, if I am remembering correctly. A lot has happened today. Calling Sydney was awful. I felt sick about the robbery."

She closed her eyes and in spite of the headache, went over the events of the day.

Every conversation. How did they go? Is it something I said or didn't say? No, someone else said it. Jaden bit her bottom lip. She would have to write down what she remembered saying during every conversation from the time Hal and Enrique called her up to look at the robbery.

"That happens to me, too. That's why we always record important interviews. I can go back over what was said, and I can also prove what was said. It's not legally valid, of course, but it's a big help. Often just enough to prove to someone what they did say. You'll probably remember about three a.m. That's what happens to me." He slowed the car at Fifth and pulled to the side of the curb in front of A Slice of Carmel's glass window and the entrance to Dolores Court.

What they did not notice was a blue Toyota parked at the end of the block. The man and the woman in the car watched as McKenzie held the door open for Jaden.

The dark haired woman walked slowly up the stairs with McKenzie at her side.

 At her door Jaden pulled her keys from the side pocket of her purse. Before she could put the key in the lock, McKenzie slipped his arm around her waist and turned her to face him. He kissed her slowly and gently. Mind whirling, she returned his kiss. She felt comfortable in his arms and really did not want him to leave. Jaden pulled away and sighed, shaking her head. "Thank you for the beautiful evening, McKenzie."

"You are very welcome, Jaden Steele." He smiled down at her.

Heart pounding, she unlocked the door. "Good night," she said in a whisper.

"Good night. Don't forget to turn that deadbolt. I won't leave until you do."

She entered the apartment and with trembling hands clicked the deadbolt shut.

Jaden leaned against the door, breathing hard, grateful that he made no move to enter.

Her feelings about him clashed in her mind. She did not believe involvement with anyone right now would help her. Jaden set her purse on the kitchen table, checking to make certain her small Monarch knife was still in the side pocket. Brent gave her this knife, custom made to a model of her right hand. She almost always carried it, except where it was not allowed. She had fallen in love with a Forge de Laquoile limited edition knife that her husband also bought. The acrylic handle was embedded with small roses. Brent's favorite knife maker made the Monarch just for her. The small knife was very inconspicuous for her to carry and fit into the palm of her hand. She had even practiced throwing with the knife and found she could be very accurate. Jaden yawned. She needed sleep to rid herself of the pounding above her eyes.

The couple in the Toyota watched the lawyer return to his car and leave.

"I thought he might stay," the general commented. "Jaden is very attractive."

"She was badly burned by that womanizing expert, Sergio. I don't think she wants any relationship right now. McKenzie would be a hard one to resist, though. He has everything--manners, intelligence, and is financially secure."

The general suspected that Bobbi might also be speaking for herself. "She needs to move on with her life." Edward Stennis spoke from bitter experience. He did not say anything more, but his pale blue eyes glanced at her in a way that made Bobbi feel as though he were reading her mind.

"I'm not going to follow him because I believe Jaden is the one in danger. You, too, for that matter. Can you show me the narrow ledge area in back of the apartments?"

"Yes. We'll have to be really quiet, though."

Once inside her apartment, Bobbi opened the kitchen window that faced the narrow outside ledge. The general leaned out. "Child's play for anyone who wants to break in. And Jaden's apartment is on the corner with a window facing the street, too. Easy to tell when she is home."

He pulled himself up onto the outside ledge.

Edward noted the window next to Bobbi's into Jaden's apartment. The corner apartment was doubly accessible because anyone agile could also reach her window from the street. This was not likely because someone on the street or driving by would certainly notice.

The general felt something on his leg and reached down to brush it off. He pulled his hand up and with it a thread. His mouth went open because the thread was taut. He groaned. In the old days he never would have tripped up like this. His heart drummed heavily.

He had not brought a weapon with him anyway. *Time to retire.*

This was not the Middle East, where he might have triggered a bomb. This was a sleepy tourist town, population around 4,000, and a third of them worked at art galleries, another third in Carmel's many restaurants.

Too late he tried to hold onto the window and jump back in Bobbi's apartment.

A man was walking toward him. He was a tall man, but all the general could see was the drawn handgun pointing directly at him.

"Don't move," the man ordered in a low, controlled voice. "Don't move until I tell you."

No chance of that. The general was frozen with anger at himself.

"Bill! No!" Bobbi gasped from her kitchen.

The policeman was distracted for a moment. In the old days the general knew he would have had time to disarm him. Now he had doubts about his ability to confront an obviously strong, athletic man holding a gun. The man's dark eyes flashed in the moonlight as he whispered, "I am a police officer. Hands against the wall. Who are you? What do you want?" He used one hand to pat the general's sides, searching for weapons.

"My name is Edward Stennis, You can look at my wallet." the General said quietly. "I'm Esther's son. I spoke to you on the phone."

Bill's mouth dropped open in genuine surprise. "General Stennis." He lowered the gun. "What are you doing here?"

"Obviously giving an impression of an old bull in a china shop. Could we go inside? Jaden has probably heard the commotion by now." He let the situation and the women distract him, too. He knew better. He was trained better. Don't take your emotions to work. Time for another old saying. *There's no fool like an old fool.*

Bill nodded. Breathing heavily, the general swung himself back into Bobbi's small kitchen. This was not good for his heart. The younger man swung himself in with no effort. General Stennis felt more envious of the man's age than his abilities. What was he? Early forties? Time is the precious element in the universe. Why does it fly away? Suddenly you wake up missing a decade.

The policeman took in Bobbi's clothes with a shocked expression on his face.

"The latest fashion?"

Bobbi grinned. Her face, even without makeup, was beautiful. She had perfect skin and her golden flecked eyes turned up slightly at the corners in an almond shape, like a cat's eyes. "This is the bag lady look."

"Yes, it is," Bill responded, realizing that she was a very beautiful woman. It was her eyes.

"What did you tie at the end of those threads?" General Stennis asked.

"A small Christmas jingle bell was for this apartment. Jaden's is a water glass. I thought the crash would wake me if necessary. I've been sleeping wearing this holster. Of course a person has to trip or move the thread. It isn't the perfect system. I've been patrolling the apartments and court a lot. Except for firing range practice I did not even wear this gun until July."

"Keep it on," the general advised. "There's a vicious killer here."

"I am glad he did not succeed with your mother," Bobbi said. "When Edward told me she was alive, I was so happy. Why didn't you and Jaden confide in me?"

"I made inquiries about everyone here before I came. Your case was so notorious that I studied it. I went to her first instead of you, Bill. Bobbi reminded me of someone I knew who had a real talent for disguise. We were practicing it tonight following Jaden and McKenzie on their date. They naively thought they were alone."

Bill frowned. He breathed deeply and exhaled slowly, as though he were angry.

Bobbi wondered if he was annoyed by not being included, or jealous because of Jaden. Of course that was it. Bill obviously liked her.

"You were painting," General Stennis said.

Bill's frown deepened and his face reddened. He looked at the paint splotches on his hands. He could not paint without spilling half the paint on himself. And it was hard to clean off.

"You are Aram," Bobbi half accused and half questioned. "You've never said anything."

"You paint every evening between seven and eleven," General Stennis told him.

Although his face turned a deeper red, William Aram Amirkhanian said nothing.

"I told you I was studying everyone. Someone here has killed two people and they have tried to kill my mother. They won't get away with what they have done. I'm trying to be logical, but what happened to my mother has made me furious."

Bobbi believed Esther's son. If the man discovered the identity of the murderer, the killer would be in danger.

"I've been studying everyone involved in this case, too," Bill told them. "So far I've only eliminated six people and two of them are dead."

"Who did you cross off your list?" Bobbi asked, curiosity driving

"You, for one. You'd have to be crazy to start killing people here after what you've been through. I would cheerfully murder whoever cut that picture of the lone cypress out of its frame. Jaden is not a killer, although she would protect herself with her skill with knives. And Enrique. He takes the bus from Salinas. Doesn't own a car. I am the fourth one. I know I did not kill anyone."

"How about Sydney and Kyle?"

"They knew the value of the painting. Maybe they stole it for insurance."

"They don't need the money," General Stennis assured them.

Bobbi stared at him. *He must know every penny that I have in the bank, too.*

The ringing of the phone split the air. The three of them looked at each other before Bobbi decided to answer on the sixth ring.

"Hello." She lifted her hand to signal them to be quiet. They complied immediately.

"Hello, Jaden. No. I'm fine. Maybe you heard someone on the street, or my television. I'm sorry," she lied. "It's probably too loud. The noise is company for me."

"No. I had a really quiet night and I'm fine. Don't worry. I'll see you in the morning."

She hung up, "I don't know if she'll believe me. I hope she doesn't come over. I'm still wearing these clothes. Jaden should have guessed quickly. Normally she is an extremely observant person. The murders have everyone upset."

"I don't want us all to work at cross purposes." Bill sat down at Bobbi's table. "General, can we come to some agreement on how to watch Jaden and Bobbi? And how is Esther? Any better?"

"Yes, she is. Talking again. She wanted so much to live to be a hundred and is really mad at whoever tried to spoil her plan. In another day or so it's really going to be hard to keep her down. I've explained that she died temporarily and must keep hidden. Mom doesn't think she knows anything about the killer. Obviously, the killer thinks differently." General Stennis rubbed the side of his head as though it hurt.

"What if I take the responsibility for Jaden and you watch Bobbi?" Bill suggested. "That way we would not be duplicating our efforts."

"Good idea. Why don't I become Bobbi's long lost uncle, here to play tourist, or maybe looking to retire. That is mostly true anyway. I'm going to retire next year and this is a beautiful retirement area. Mom doesn't want to return to the East Coast so I've really been thinking about moving here. To be honest they can keep the east coast. Hot in the summer, snow in the winter."

"You need another name," Bobbi offered.

"Don't worry about that. I have plenty of different identity cards." The general grinned. "From the old days. Now they've made me a pencil pusher and it's boring."

Bill knew that General Stennis was very well connected or he would not have produced a personal physician for his mother and two guards for her hospital room. When he pushed pencils things still happened. He had to be in his early sixties. He was in excellent physical condition.

"Where are you going to stay?" Bobbi asked.

"Right here," Edward Stennis answered. "This looks like a sofa bed. I can't do much if I'm off in a hotel somewhere. After all, you want to save Uncle Edward some money, don't you? And this way I'll be near Jaden when you are away, Bill. The ladies will have their own bodyguard."

Bobbi's beautiful cat-like eyes narrowed. Then she smiled. "Well, I have been really nervous after Sergio's murder, and I thought finding old Jonah in the park was the last straw. Then the attempt on your mother's life. This will protect me in two ways."

"How's that?" Bill asked.

"I'll have a witness to my movements."

"Good. *That's settled.* My motel room is booked for tonight so I'll check out in the morning. Expect Uncle to walk you to work."

"Thank you for coming, General," Bill said. "I'm not going to tell anybody at all, even at work. It seems hard to keep secrets around here. Someone is reporting to the mayor. Only the three of us and Esther will know who you are until we solve this mystery in this village."

Bill left by the window. "If Jaden hears your door open and close, she is going to be right out, Bobbi. She's on her guard, too."

"I'd better do the same thing, then," the general said. "I'll leave through the side window."

"Thank you for everything." Bobbi looked down at her shoes and then lifted her eyes to meet the general's. "I like those disguises. It's like my acting days in college. I'm going to try several. I'm sure neither Jaden nor McKenzie recognized me. It's fun."

"It's usually not a game, Bobbi." The general's fingers closed around her arm tightly. "Promise me you won't do anything without telling me. When I see you again, I want to know if you or Jaden is holding anything back that might help solve the murders. I know you've both been playing detectives. You and Jaden are sharp enough to have discovered something, even if you don't realize it."

Bobbi's face flushed when she thought of Jonah's notebook. She nodded silently.

He must be some kind of a mind reader because she felt guilt pop out all over her like hives. Edward must be able to see it. But Jaden had the notebook. She could not ask for it without telling her about this man and who he was. Copies of the notebook pages were in her folder, though. Tomorrow she would show him all the information she had on the case. Another mind, one used to solving puzzles, would help.

Jaden felt so revived in the cool, bright autumn morning that she wished the apartment had a balcony where she could enjoy her coffee and watch the barking seagulls flying toward the water. Looking out the window she wondered if somehow balconies could be built, but the roof of the next building nestled next to theirs. Her thoughts went to McKenzie, his kiss, and her reaction to it. He was so likeable. "Now is not the time for me to become involved with anyone," she muttered to herself, knowing she was right. This was the first morning in forever that she had not thought of her husband, Brent. She usually woke up, felt for him in the bed next to her. The bed was empty. Her chest ached when she realized he would never be there.

Because her apartment was on the corner, her living room window had a view of part of the park at the Ocean and Mission corner. Some people were constructing a scarecrow, probably more than one, in preparation for the Oktoberfest celebration. There would be food and entertainment. She would ask McKenzie if he would like to take her.

She poured a second cup of coffee and wondered about the unusually loud television program Bobbi had watched last night. That was the first time the librarian had ever turned the volume up so high. She did not even like most television programming. Like a good librarian, her friend preferred to read. Jaden left her old television in Nebraska. *Bobbi must really be worried or nervous. I am, too. We must solve this case before another tragedy materializes.*

What would be good for breakfast? Jaden decided on a slice of cantaloupe. She had bought one at the Farmer's Market in Monterey. It smelled delicious as the blade sliced into it. She rinsed off the knife and was drying it when she stopped and stared. *Knives cut.* What was it about cutting? Of course, two people had been stabbed to death, the first two murders in Carmel in years. Maybe that was what was lurking in the back of her mind. Again she tried to remember conversations with people yesterday. Jaden could not record all her conversations. She should take notes as soon as possible after an important conversation. Memories fade quickly.

Jaden stared at the painting on her wall. The painting of Nebraska cornfields as far as the eye could see belonged to her grandparents. Certainly it was not a valuable painting. It meant the world to her because of the memory of her caring grandma and grandpa.

If anyone cut it out of the frame, she would be devastated. She blinked, suddenly aware of what had been eluding her all evening. "I need to talk to Bobbi."

The woman must already be at the library because no one answered.

"I'll call her from work." Heart racing, Jaden threw on clothes and for makeup two slashes of burgundy lipstick. She was unlocking the shop when she spotted someone out of the corner of her eye. This was the customer who had admired the swords. He carried a small black travel bag and he was heading for the stairway to the apartments.

"Sir. Edward," she called. "May I help you?"

The tall man turned and smiled at her. "Oh, no thank you."

"There's no one at home today in any of the apartments." She began to feel uneasy about him.

He smiled at her. "I am really sorry. I should have introduced myself when I was in your excellent store. Your inventory is so fascinating. My name is Edward Jones and I am Roberta's uncle. I'll be staying with her for a few days." A wave of guilt about lying washed over him.

He blamed it on developing a conscience away from DC.

Jaden stared at him, not quite believing his words. He seemed so open and honest. He was one of those men, like Hal, who became more attractive as they grew older. Why had Bobbi not said something about an uncle visiting?

Edward Stennis fought to maintain his casual demeanor in front of the beautiful, intelligent young woman who could never play poker. Disbelief was written all over her face, and for good reason. He thought of how controlled Bobbi's face would have been in such a situation, just like Lisette's. Edward swallowed hard. Lisette was gone, and part of him died with her. Unlike Jaden Steele, Roberta Petra Schmidt would make an excellent spy.

"She gave me the key and I'm going to meet her for lunch," he told Jaden. "She's been so distracted she no doubt forgot to mention my coming. Would you like to join us for lunch? It's very simple. No trouble to have you."

The woman obviously relaxed a little but Edward knew that she would call Bobbi as soon as she had the chance. She sensed something wrong about him. Jaden's instincts were good.

"No, thank you, Mr. Jones. I have to run the store today. The man who usually works with me, Hal, is helping decorate the park for the Oktoberfest. He said he would give me a break at the shop from five to eight."

The General doubted that this Oktoberfest would be flowing with beer, as it would in

Germany, for a real Oktoberfest. "That ought to be a nice celebration. The weather is beautiful. Bobbi needs to get out. I'll take her. I hope you join us."

"Thank you. I'll have to see. I'm also waiting for some information about a robbery that took place here two nights ago."

"Bobbi told me. I believe she was extremely nervous about everything that's happened. She has suffered enough. That's why she invited me to visit for a few days. "

Jaden took a deep breath. That was understandable. She felt apprehensive herself. Bobbi's background would make her a lot warier. Jaden wished she had a relative to call. There was no one in her family left. Her eyes misted over. She realized she was feeling sorry for herself and wanted to leave the company of Edward Jones immediately.

"I'll talk to Bobbi later." She whirled and went back into the shop.

Once back in the store, Jaden wiped her eyes and blew her nose. Annoyance that Bobbi had not called her about Uncle Edward prompted her to call the library right away. Something about Edward did not seem right.

"Jaden," Bobbi answered. "Yes, I should have told you. Uncle Edward wrote that he wanted to visit the Monterey Bay area, play a little golf, and after everything that has happened, I jumped at the chance to invite him to stay. He'll be here about a week. Maybe a little longer."

"There's something I wanted to go over with you. Do you have some time today to bring your notes over?"

"What is it?"

"I'm almost certain that I know who stole the painting. Not absolute. I need more proof."

"Jaden, don't tell me over the phone. I was going to have lunch with Uncle Edward. I'll call him and tell him to go out by himself."

"Thanks, Bobbi."

At lunchtime Jaden closed the store. Eating a turkey sandwich in her apartment, she went over her notes carefully and found more than one error she had missed. A note read that Marian Martelli had said that Sydney paid $1,200 for the Aram painting. Sydney told her he paid $2000. Could he have been mistaken? *Not Sydney.* He paid the $2,000. What happened to the difference? She could ask Bill directly what he had received for the painting. He had never admitted that he was the artist. What would the gallery charge for a fee? The commission on $1,200 would be a lot less than the commission on $2,000.

She guessed commissions were fifty per cent. Suspicion was beginning to nag at her that Sergio, who was alive at that time, and constantly spent beyond his means, might have pocketed the difference. Aram may have found out, giving him a motive. Would the artist kill for $800? People have certainly been killed for less.

If it happened several times, though, there would be a much larger sum involved.

Now the painting was worth ten times its original price. What would The Lone Cypress sell for to a covetous private collector who may have actually ordered it?

Jaden glanced over to see the corner of the park across from the children's and local history library branch. People were beginning to come to the Oktoberfest booths.

There probably would not be a parking place in town. I think I should keep the store open until nine to try to catch some of that tourist trade. She hoped Hal would come over to give her a break, but, even if he could not make it, Jaden decided to leave the store open.

Bobbi came over at one-thirty with her notes.

They sat at Jaden's desk while she went over what she suspected. "Everything leads back to the gallery, doesn't it? Have you heard from Vincent about the insurance?"

"No. It's strange. I've been thinking about calling the gallery again. Sydney needs that information. Maybe Vincent hasn't returned."

"Jaden. You have to be careful. I'm going to ask Uncle Edward to keep an eye on you. There's been too much going on for you not to be cautious at all times."

"I can take care of myself."

"How?"

"Well, I'm carrying a knife in my pocket."

Bobbi's golden flecked, almond shaped eyes narrowed. "Do you think that's going to protect you? What if the killer surprises you?"

Jaden's deep violet-blue eyes met hers. Bobbi had a point. She did not know how to answer. She had practiced with the knife, and it handled very well. Her desire to demonstrate was controlled by her knowledge that Bobbi hated knives.

For good reason.

Jaden was raised with knives, taught how to handle them, how to make them, and appreciated their value. Our ancestors invented the much needed tool, first using bone or rock honed to the right shape. What pioneer could have ever gone without a knife? It was warped people who used them to intimidate and kill. Jaden had taken self-defense classes and classes on handling knives.

That's where she met Brent.

Anxious to change the subject, she told Bobbi, "I want to see those gallery records of the sale to Sydney. Vincent should have them by now. It's almost three. He should have at least called if there were a problem. I'll call the gallery right now."

The number rang nine times before Jaden hung up. "They don't have an answering machine? That seems strange. What business does not have answering service?"

"Sometimes those aren't working correctly or they just forget to turn it on."

"I never forget the machine here. It's good business to have an answering service or voice mail or some way for customers to contact you. Maybe it is just broken."

"My uncle and I will walk down to the gallery. Is Enrique here?"

"Yes, He's upstairs sweeping the walkway outside the apartments."

"I'm going to ask him to come downstairs and watch the store and you while we're gone. If only Kyle and Sydney would get back and open up 'The Mad Hatter's' again."

"That's not necessary. But thank you for worrying about my safety."

"Jaden, it is necessary."

She watched as Bobbi went back up the concrete stairs.

Several customers came into the store to keep Jaden busier than normal. She knew she was right about keeping the store open, maybe until nine p.m. If only Kyle and Sydney would come back. This would have been a good day for the café.

During breaks she called the Martelli and Howard Gallery two more times with the same result. Maybe something was wrong with their answering machine. If there were a break in customers, she would ask Gene in the California Gallery if he knew anything about Sergio's gallery closing. Galleries abounded in Carmel, but everyone always seemed to know what everyone else was doing. The well-known town was small townish in many ways. The word-of-mouth news network was as active as the internet.

At four p.m. McKenzie walked into his office in downtown San Diego.

The receptionist at the front desk looked up with an expression of surprise on her face. "Mr. Anderson, I didn't think you would be back from Monterey until next week."

"Luanne, I received a message at my hotel that I was needed here right away. I took a flight from Monterey airport at one."

The woman shook her head. "I didn't call you. Let me contact Pat and see if he did." Pat was his law clerk and secretary. "There might be some problem that he thought needed your attention right away. Maybe something I did not know about."

Some extraordinary problem might make him call. Usually everything went through Luanne.

"Call him," McKenzie said. "I'll go in and check through the mail. Is there anything else?"

"No. Everyone knew you said you were coming back next week. How is Petra?"

"Doing well in spite of the murders. She and everyone else are nervous." McKenzie thought of his golden-eyed client. She was a nice, intelligent woman who did not deserve what happened to her. He smiled with satisfaction when he saw the look on the Assistant District Attorney's face when the not guilty verdict was returned.

Luanne had already opened the mail, and had excellent judgment, but McKenzie always looked through each piece before it went into the round file. The mail went into three other trays. 1. Immediate action by phone call or e-mail. 2. Action by regular mail. 3. Can wait and answer appropriately in good time. He had to admit that if he knew the people involved, his answer was usually based on whether he liked them or not. McKenzie knew how unprofessional that was.

Concentrating was difficult because his mind kept wandering back to the previous night's dinner with Jaden. She, like Bobbi, had had a bad time in her life. Jaden was an intelligent beauty with that dark hair, white skin, and unusual deep violet-blue eyes. She had a vulnerable streak in her that Sergio Martelli no doubt spotted and used to his advantage. Jaden and Petra both want to clear their names. McKenzie knew that neither one of them was a murderer.

Luanne knocked on the side of the open door. "You don't look that interested in your mail."

"I'm not. And I'm tired."

"Pat says he did not call you."

McKenzie stared at her. An icy stab almost robbed him of his voice when he thought of Jaden and of Petra. "Excuse me, Luanne. I need to call someone right now."

He picked up the phone and punched in Jaden's number. No answer. He called the store and finally got an answering machine. "Your call is very important to us. If you will leave a message we will return your call as soon as possible." He left a message.

"Luanne," He called, realizing that there was only one reason for the phone call; to get rid of him. "Can you get me the phone number for the Carmel Police Department?"

Bobbi called at five, "The gallery is closed."

"Thanks, Bobbi. It's strange."

Around six she decided to take a dinner break. She visited the California Gallery. Gene Miller, the gallery owner and the one employee, told her, "No. I haven't heard that they were closing for a while. They've probably had a hard time since Sergio," he gulped, "was killed. Sergio was the go-getter, in more ways than one. I've always wondered why Vincent stayed there."

Jaden frowned. "Why wouldn't he stay? He is half owner of the gallery."

"Well, of course you wouldn't know. Happened a few years back."

"What happened?" Jaden's heart began to pound heavily. She already well knew the type of trouble Sergio created. His self-indulgence led him to seduce as many women as possible. He thought it was normal.

Gene told her. "Vincent's wife."

Jaden groaned to herself, really not needing to hear anything more.

"He had a knack with women and no scruples at all. They were all fair game."

Jaden felt her face reddening but she rooted her feet to the tile floor. As much as she hated being reminded of her own stupidity, she had to know everything Gene would tell her.

"Not Vincent's wife and Sergio?" Jaden whispered, wondering at her own stupidity.

"Oh, it was the talk of the town for a few months. And that foolish woman thought Sergio would dump his wife and marry her."

All Jaden could do was sigh.

"He had it too good with Marian who seemed to be unusually tolerant of whatever her hubby did. I don't know how she could have ignored it."

"She didn't know?"

"Nobody's that unaware," Gene answered. "Then of course there was that horrible accident at the beach."

"Accident?" Jaden knew what he was going to say before he said it.

"Poor thing drowned at Carmel beach. Vincent was never quite the same after her death.

We all thought he would leave town. I'm surprised he stayed. Maybe all of his money was in the gallery. I never would have stayed in partnership with a man like Sergio Martelli. Rumors flew around town. Some say she walked into the ocean after Sergio refused to marry her. Some say Vincent killed her in a rage. Others said Marian finally took some action. Nobody would have blamed either one of them."

"At Carmel beach?" Jaden felt numb. She realized that Jonah might have seen that supposed "drowning." Incidents flew like pieces in a puzzle in her mind. The last few pieces were fitting into the dark, irregular spaces.

"Vincent was devastated. Went away for two months, some say for treatment. The big surprise for all of us was that he came back to Carmel and stayed with the gallery. Now some say he's got a perfect chance with Marian. Great revenge, if you ask me."

Jaden nodded.

An older couple came into the gallery to talk to Gene about an oil painting of an old barn and farm scene that was in the window.

"That's a Morris Pace. Very popular California artist of the nineteenth century." Gene was beginning his casual sales pitch. "Brings great auction prices."

Jaden waved at him and left. With Gene's gossip running through her mind, she totally forgot to call McKenzie. Distracted, she walked over to the park to join the lively crowd at the Oktoberfest and to buy something to eat. The smell of food in the air made her stomach rumble. She decided on a plate of bratwurst, red cabbage, and a boiled potato that looked good on several passing plates.

As Jaden stepped up to the booth, Bill appeared beside her.

"May I buy you dinner?" He asked with a pleasant smile on his face. Bill was trying his best to be casual. Bill knew Jaden had not realized that he had followed her from the court. He watched her go from her shop to the California Gallery for some reason. She was in there about twenty minutes and left with an almost dazed look on her face. He followed her easily. Bill also was trying to tuck the feeling he had for this beautiful young woman into the back of his mind. He was not a portrait artist, but in front of him was a portrait he would love to paint. Those dark, unruly curls and the deep blue-violet eyes. Maybe it was that breathtaking full moon in the sky that was getting to him. And, naturally, she already had a friend, that lawyer, McKenzie Anderson. The ones he liked always seemed to be married or attached.

Jaden smiled at him. "Are you the park security now? Looks like a peaceful crowd."

He nodded. "Well, there are only four of us and the chief is on vacation."

The man behind the booth counter, wearing a white apron, waited for their order.

"Thank you, Bill. I'd like the wurst and red cabbage. I love red cabbage."

"I'll have the same." He pulled out his wallet and paid for their dinners.

They carried their plates to a table to get their utensils and napkins. The table also had several varieties of mustard in small packages.

"Not like one big jug," Bill commented, choosing a spicy brown mustard.

"This is Carmel, after all. Five types of mustard for a picnic." Jaden put a packet of spicy mustard and another of garlic mustard on her plate, then turned to look for a free space at one of the paper covered picnic tables.

"Over there," Bill pointed with one hand in the direction of the end of a table.

"Thank you for dinner, Bill." She slid onto the picnic table bench.

"My pleasure," he said truthfully. This was also the best way to watch her, and his desire to find out more about her was overwhelming. He sat directly opposite Jaden at the table.

"I'd ask how you were doing, but I feel as though it would be like asking someone how their voyage was on the Titanic." Bill lifted a forkful of red cabbage.

"Now that you mention it, it does seem like a lot has gone wrong since I came to Carmel." She spoke casually but her mind whirled with a combination of fear and guilt. "I keep wondering if it's somehow my fault." Her voice wavered. "When I found this cutlery store on the internet, I thought I was the luckiest person. Now I feel just the opposite." Self-pity washed over her like an ocean wave.

Bill did not comment, which made her feel even worse. She felt his silence meant he agreed.

"At least Esther is better. She'll want to come back from the dead soon. The physician her son sent has left."

"I'm so thankful."

"I want Esther to stay out of sight until this case is solved. Not certain what she'll want to do. She's quite an old gal." He sliced his sausage and popped a piece into his mouth. "That's good. Tastes even better than it smells cooking."

"Could I ask you something?" Jaden decided to be direct. She saw the reflection of the full moon in his dark, curious eyes. "Why haven't you told anyone that you are an artist?"

He appeared startled for a moment. Bill remembered that Jaden had been in his apartment and if he had left his spare bedroom door open, she certainly would have seen his studio. "It's a private part of my life."

"But you are an outstanding, well-known artist. When I saw your paintings in Sergio's gallery, I loved them. You should be proud of your talent."

"It's hard to explain. It's difficult for others to understand. I need a spot to be alone and paint. Interruptions break into my work."

She stared at him.

Bill swallowed hard. Those unusual deep blue eyes fixed on him. He wanted to go over to her and kiss her. The same feeling swept over him when he first met her at Kyle and Sydney's. He had met and dated many beautiful women, but he had never found one so intriguing. Some of them were so shallow that they tried to find out his income before they decided if they were interested. *I can't let my feelings for Jaden interfere with guarding her.* Obviously, that successful attorney is after her. Why would she want a moody artist when she could have a steady, successful man like McKenzie Anderson?

"Your paintings are wonderful, Bill. You should be proud of them."

"I am." He could kick himself because he had just told her that he wanted to be alone to paint. But that was the truth. She needed to hear that right away.

"Have you always painted?"

"Sketched a lot, even when I was young. I have notebooks of sketches going back about twenty-two years. Then the police work was getting to me and I took some art classes at a local night school. It became a passion. After a rotten day dealing with ugly people, I could focus on painting a beautiful scene on canvas. The world is beautiful. I believe that if more people saw that, there would be less crime. Criminals don't see beyond their immediate passions. So many times people don't look up to see what is right in front of their eyes."

Jaden closed her eyes and opened them. For a few moments she had the odd sensation that they were the only two people in the park. They were surrounded by people talking and a band playing German music "I understand," she answered in almost a whisper. "Those large paintings. The larger they are, the more beauty to block out ugliness caused by some people."

Amazed that she understood the reason behind the large canvases, he cleared his throat to restore his lost voice. He always had trouble talking about his art. It was like talking about a lover. Some men did. He always thought that was in the worst possible taste.

"When I asked at the gallery if you ever did anything small, Vincent said no."

"That was curious you should ask. Why?"

She looked down at her empty paper plate. "I thought maybe someday I could afford a smaller painting. You had already told the gallery that you did not do smaller works. You liked the large form. Vincent said that you would not change to anything else as long as it was successful."

"He was right. I love that large form. It's hard to change."

"But not impossible."

He leaned over the table and took her hand. She closed her eyes again. Her heart was racing and her resolve to not get involved with anyone was crumbling.

The mood was broken by a ring from Bill's cell phone. He withdrew his hand to lean back and pull out his phone. He fought the desire to shut the thing off, but knew it must be an emergency call.

Jaden leaned back, too, thinking, *Saved by the bell.* She was not certain if she wanted to be saved. A deep sigh rose in her throat. What was the matter with her? *How fickle could she be? Yesterday she was wondering about her feelings for McKenzie Anderson.*

"O.K. The park's going fine. Everyone is enjoying the Oktoberfest. There are five private security people here. I'll be over as soon as possible." He slipped the phone back in its case. "There's been a robbery. I'll have to investigate."

Jaden's heart was pounding in her ears when they stood up. She could barely hear the band. Bill's food was only half eaten. He turned around to put it in one of the garbage cans behind him. An old woman shuffled out from behind the pyracantha bushes behind them. Several homeless frequented the park. As much as the woman stayed back behind the garbage can and the bush, she looked familiar. Jaden felt certain that she had seen her before, in Pacific Grove, in the alley next to Za'tar's. Bill realized what she wanted and handed her the plate. "Thanks, mister," came a rough grumble. She faded back into the bushes. Bill shook his head. "I'm going to take you back to the shop. It's right on the way. But I should go now. Sorry about this."

"You're the one who should be sorry. You only ate half your dinner."

"I can get something later. This is going to be open until ten." He put his hand on her shoulder and they walked together across Mission Street and down the two blocks to Dolores. Bill's hand had slipped into hers in what seemed to be the most natural gesture in the world.

"You made quite an impression on me," Bill smiled broadly for the first time Jaden could remember. He held out his left hand. Between the thumb and forefinger were two red marks.

Jaden's eyes narrowed. She stopped and looked at him. "It's not really funny. I'm sorry about biting you. I really thought you meant Esther harm."

"I know you did, Jaden. It's healing. And I've had my shots." Another smile.

It made him so much more attractive than the detective with the furrowed brow.

When they arrived at the plate glass windows at the left side of the entrance to the court, there were people in the courtyard visiting the two open galleries. She did not want to let go of his hand, but she had to take the keys from her purse. Some of the tourists were already coming over to enter the shop. Jaden wished they would all go away and leave her alone with Bill.

When she opened the door, the small brass bell rang softly. She keyed in the all clear sequence, barely able to remember the code.

"I'll go now and be back as soon as possible," Bill told her.

After he left, she realized that Bill had not told her which store was robbed.

His absence left an unusual void in the court. It gave her a few minutes to think. Her thoughts drifted from Bill to McKenzie and back again. She should have called McKenzie tonight. On the other hand, he normally would have called her. Where has he gone? She thought that it was a good thing he did not call tonight. She would have asked him to go to the Oktoberfest and she never would have had the conversation with Bill.

That might have been better than realizing that Bill stirred deep emotions in her that she had not felt before. She loved her husband, Brent, who, in a way, was a best friend type like McKenzie. Likeable. Easy to talk to. Very steady and good natured.

Once the store was open she started showing knives, made a few sales of the Forge de Laguoile knives, another of their good sellers, and decided that she had made the right move keeping the store open. Several people also called to ask if the store were open, and how late? Except for the tourists, and the open gallery, the court was quiet. No one was upstairs in the apartments. *This would have been such a great day for The Mad Hatter's, even if food is being sold in the park.*

Her phone rang. Hal was on the other line. "Jaden, I am sorry. Can't come over tonight. Sandy's mother in San Jose has been in an auto accident, and we're going to the hospital. We're on Highway One right now. How are you doing?"

"Fine. I've been selling to tourists pretty steadily so I'm glad about keeping the store open. The Oktoberfest is bringing in tourists. Nothing I can't handle. I'll close at nine."

"Have Kyle and Sydney returned?"

"No, but there are people around. Bill was here for a while but he had to answer a robbery call." She reached into her pocket and felt the smooth handle of her Monarch.

"Be careful. If it gets quiet, close the store," were his last words to her. "I hope she pays attention to that." Bill walked rapidly down Ocean Avenue toward the beach. He did not want to tell Jaden that the robbery was at the Martelli and Howard Gallery. His heart was booming as he half walked and half ran. He left Jaden with plenty of people around, and her special backup bodyguard, General Edward Stennis.

The startling fact that more of his paintings might be cut out of their frames made him think that if he ever found out who had done it, he could easily become a murderer himself. Each painting was like a child to him.

When he finally arrived at the gallery, breathless, he was met by the Carmel parking enforcement officer, Irene, who told him, "Looks like someone forced the door. I've looked in just as far as the door frame, calling to see if anyone was there."

"You didn't touch anything?"

"No, I didn't, but I really wanted to turn on the lights. Could be a trap."

"I'm going in."

Bill entered the gallery cautiously. "Hello. This is the police. If you can hear my voice, step out with your hands up." Silence greeted him. He unstrapped his small but powerful flashlight. This was going to make him a target. He held the end of the light as far away from him as he could. The gallery seemed empty. His sixth sense told him that he was not alone in the large room. Humans give off something that one can feel. Maybe it's the breathing that he could sense. He had great hearing. Someone else was in the gallery. And what he sensed was actually a scent, a scent he recognized when he took a deep breath. He gagged briefly. Someone could be hiding behind the desk. He would have to check there first. He must give another warning. While someone could shoot him without warning, the reverse was not true. And he thought he would never use his gun.

"I am a police officer! Come out with your hands up! There are more officers outside."

Still no response. This situation made him think of a stormy sea. He should back out of the door right now, quietly, without making more of a target of himself. He suspected that whoever was in the gallery was either ready to kill or in no shape to shoot him. No use taking chances.

The odor of the place repulsed him. It smelled like death.

Luckily, as he backed out on the street, a Carmel police car arrived.

"Irene, aren't you finished at six? Did you discover the door open yourself?"

"No, Bill. Someone reported the break-in by phone. Since we were short handed, I volunteered to come over and check. I found the door open."

Bill examined the lock on the door. Dents from blows in the wood surrounded the metal lock plate. The lock was not damaged. Nothing in the blows that he saw would break the lock so that someone could open the door. The damage was for show. The uneasy feeling in the back of his mind crept to the front. He could feel the furrows deepening on his forehead.

Irene said, "Here comes Ron."

Ron came up beside him. "What's going on?"

Bill answered in a controlled voice. "There's been a robbery, I think, but something's wrong inside the gallery. I smelled trouble."

"Let's go in," Ron said.

Both men drew their guns. Bill stepped into the gallery first. "This is the police!" he shouted. Inside the small gallery there could be no doubt about his voice carrying. Silence answered him.

Ron repeated, "We are police officers. Is anyone here? We are going to enter the building."

Silence. The gallery seemed empty, though Bill could smell a deadly familiar odor.

He pulled out his flashlight to begin a search on the left side of the room. He flashed the light under the neatly arranged desk. He looked at each of his paintings, feeling grateful that they were intact. His light at last came to rest on the doorknob of a small closet. A dark stain was seeping out under the door.

"There," Ron whispered.

Bill's stomach turned over as they advanced to the door.

"Fingerprints," Ron warned.

"The door's not closed all the way." Bill reached to the top of the door with one finger and swung the door open.

"Quick, Ron. Call the paramedics! I need to make another call."

His fingers trembled as he pushed in the number that Stennis gave him. He breathed a sigh of relief to hear an immediate, "Hello."

"Edward?" Bill heard his own voice waver.

"Yes, Bill."

"Edward, where are you?"

"At the care facility in Pacific Grove. Mom is bugging me to go home and I want her here, safe for a few more days. I left Bobbi watching Jaden. How is she?"

"There was a robbery call that I had to answer. It's the Martelli and Howard Gallery, Edward, and there's been a shooting. When I left

Jaden, she was in the store with a number of customers. I think this is a set up." He explained about the door.

"Call Jaden! Tell her to close and lock the store. Can you send a squad car?"

"Our police force is mostly here. I'll leave Ron to take care of all the details and call a forensic team in from Monterey."

The wail of a siren almost drowned his voice.

"Bill, what's happening?"

"Paramedics and ambulance."

"Can you leave?"

The paramedics rushed into the gallery. "Yes. I'll tell Ron."

"Get over to the court right away! I'll be there. Take me twenty minutes."

Bill explained quickly to his officers that he knew there was another problem in Dolores Street Court. Jaden was in danger.

"Again?" Ron asked as the ambulance crew went into the gallery.

Bill tried to call A Slice of Carmel again. He yelled into his phone for Jaden to close the store and was already running down Sixth to Dolores Street Court.

Jaden began the end of the day procedures by putting the day's receipts in the safe. She would not be able to go to the bank until Monday. Two customers remained in the shop. Jaden glanced into the center of the court and saw that same homeless woman from the park. Had she followed them here? Some of them were like puppy dogs and followed whoever had been kind to them. Others took advantage. Some had severe problems and should not be out on the streets. A wave of sadness washed through her when she thought of Mr. Jonah. She watched the woman go by the corner of the California Gallery. Maybe she planned to sleep there. Jaden hoped not.

Some tourists were milling around the court when she saw Gene close the gallery's door. While she was straightening up the counters, she wondered whatever had happened to McKenzie. It finally occurred to her to check the phone messages. Maybe Vincent had called. What ever happened to him? *Vincent.* She gulped. *Of course.*

With trembling hands she helped the two customers left in the store. One bought a ceramic vegetable peeler and a small pair of scissors.

"Interesting shop," one of the women said. "Nothing like this in Lincoln."

"Are you from Nebraska?" Jaden asked. "I'm from Kearny. I've been here about nine months."

"We live in Lincoln. How lucky you are to be in such a lovely spot," one of the women told her. "The ocean is so beautiful."

"I wanted a change," Jaden answered. Not the terror that followed. A wave of longing for home and safety washed over her.

When they left, Jaden finally played back the messages. One was from McKenzie saying that he had unexpectedly been called back to San Diego. "Take care, Jaden. Please, you and Petra be extra careful. I'll be back as soon as I can."

Kyle's voice. "We're in Bishop. We'll be home in a day, dear."

McKenzie called again. He sounded hesitant, not at all like his regular, pleasant self. "Jaden, I'm not certain about this, but I have some very bad feelings. No one from my office called me.

Either someone got the message wrong or the message was sent deliberately. I suspect that's what happened and I'm really worried."

The next message was from Hal. "Jaden. I'm sorry I didn't get over to the shop. This is a false alarm. Sandy's mother is fine. Someone probably thought they were being funny, but it was a cruel joke. I won't be able to work until tomorrow some time. It'll be eleven-thirty by the time we get back to Carmel."

Jaden stared at the case of swords and Grandpa Abel's knife. One message sent in error might be a mistake. Two was too much of a coincidence. She swallowed hard.

The next message was from a breathless Bill. "No time to explain. If you get this at the store, lock it immediately. I'm on my way but it will take me a few minutes."

"Please! Right now! Lock the store!" The message vibrated in her ears.

Because she heard panic in a voice that normally was controlled, a sense of doom gripped her. Whatever happened at the gallery was as bad as murder. It could not be. *No...Not another murder!* Pulling the keys from her pocket, she moved to lock the deadbolt. Her movement made the bell attached to the door ring. An unfamiliar sound, a slight scuffle made her gasp. *I didn't keep track of the customers!* She did not see anyone in the store. At closing they usually checked the small bathroom. That noise again indicated movement. Jaden realized that although she could not see anyone, she was not alone. Pure fright triggered a flight response. For a few seconds her feet would not cooperate. She moved to unlock the front door and escape into the court.

Too late. The bathroom door opened. She turned, expecting to see Vincent.

Marian Martelli stepped out of the room holding a small handgun. "Hello, Jaden."

The woman smiled a smile that made her look like a Halloween jack-o-lantern.

"Stop! Don't move!" Marian shrieked.

Jaden's heart accelerated until she trembled. "I'm not moving, Marian." Sergio's wife could not be the murderer, but here she was, glaring at Jaden with glazed eyes and a voice full of hate. All Jaden could think of was an inane, "Marian, is something wrong?" *Dumb question of the year.*

"You know, you tramp!"

"No, I don't," Jaden lied. She desperately wanted to keep Marian talking. "Why are you here? Should I call your sister, Abby? Maybe Vincent could help."

"He took Sergio from me! First, all of those little tramps, like you and Vincent's stupid wife! Then he killed my Sergio. Well, he's sorry and you will be, too. You are going to die in a robbery. Open the safe!"

Jaden was a communications expert without a word to say. She forced herself to speak in a normal voice, "Marian, you don't want to do this. Vincent killed Sergio."

One look at Marian's pale white face and wild eyes told Jaden she was at this moment capable of anything. As crazed as the woman looked now, Jaden could not believe she stabbed Sergio and Jonah or broke into Kyle and Sydney's apartment to steal that painting. Vincent did that.

Marian said "he." Suddenly Jaden realized everything that had happened and searched for words, "Marian, you didn't steal 'The Lone Cypress,' did you?"

Marian blinked her eyes. She stared at Jaden until her bright eyes narrowed to slits. "Steal the Aram painting?"

"Yes, did you steal the painting from Kyle and Sydney's apartment? Did Vincent tell you about the customer who wanted it?"

"No."

"Vincent stole it. For the money."

"Yes." She laughed hysterically. "He's very sorry now."

"Marian, where is Vincent? He was going to bring me information on the stolen painting for Sydney." Thinking the woman was distracted, Jaden took a step forward.

"Get back! He won't bring you anything, ever! I shot him." She waved the gun.

Jaden froze. Her heart was racing. She could barely control her trembling hands. "Vincent stole the painting. It's probably at your storage facility in Monterey."

"He said we could have a lot of money. He said Sergio bankrupted the business. Vincent could fix everything." Her voice broke. "He said

Sergio did not care about me. He was a liar. Sergio was my world. He took Sergio from me. What can I do now?"

"Vincent killed Sergio, and Mr. Jonah."

Marian's wailed pitifully, "What am I going to do without Sergio?"

"You are making a mistake." Why had she never blamed her husband?

"No mistake. Vincent said you and that Bobbi were too close to the truth."

"Marian, you called McKenzie Anderson and Hal, didn't you?"

"First we had to get rid of most of the people who lived in the court. Vincent planned the robbery of your store to kill you. He thought I would marry him. What a fool. Sergio was my love, my only love."

Abby was right. For Marian, love was blind. Sergio stole money and cheated on her and she calls him her world.

"Vincent killed the homeless man, Jonah. That tramp tried to blackmail Vincent about his wife's death and seeing him go into the parking garage at the time Sergio was killed."

"I know," Jaden answered quietly, realizing Marian would never believe she did not know about their marriage. "I understand. And Esther?"

"Vincent said the nosy old lady was researching us. He said you were chasing Sergio."

Jaden's heart boomed so loudly that she could barely hear the hysterical woman.

"He did not want you! He always came back to me! Why did you come here?"

Jaden slipped her hand into her pocket and felt the Monarch knife. The narrow blade would not do much against a gun. For some reason Brent's voice echoed in her ears. *You have the advantage of surprise. No one would expect you to use a knife as well as you do.*

With no warning at all, the sound of pounding at the courtside plate glass window distracted Marian. That homeless woman from the park was beating on the window with some heavy object. Both women looked, but Jaden swiftly drew out the small knife that she had been clutching. She had never thrown at a person before. The narrow, stainless steel blade snapped open, Jaden focused all of her attention, and threw. Marian, slightly slower in turning away from the noise at the window, whirled and fired.

Jaden dived to the floor toward the door. Her ears rang with the explosion of the shot and the crash of the glass display case shattering in the small space.

Marian screamed and slumped to the floor. The knife caught her right shoulder.

With glass flying all around her, Jaden dove for the spinning gun, swooped it up, and dove again for the key in the lock of the shop door. Her blood-splattered arms stung. She wrenched the key to the left and yanked the door open. The bag woman barreled her way into the store. "Jaden!"

That crazy woman was screaming in the voice of Bobbi Jones!

Marian's wails sounded like a wounded animal's as she thrashed in the glass on the floor.

"Bobbi?" Jaden gasped. "Bobbi? You?" Marian's screams drowned her voice.

The bag woman hugged her.

"She was going to shoot me and make it look like a robbery. I threw the knife. The first person I ever targeted."

Jaden wanted to scream herself. Blood oozed down her arms. Strangely, they did not hurt.

"I know. I know. Did you realize how quick you were with that knife?" She pulled a rag from her pants pocket and put it on one of Jaden's bleeding arms. "Let me get some paper towels and I'll take you out of here," she yelled over Marian's screeching.

With gun drawn, Bill ran into the store. "Jaden! You're…you're safe!"

"I called 911 when I saw this," Bobbi said, prying the gun from Jaden's fingers.

"The police are not going to believe another call to this court."

The room swirled around Jaden. She grabbed the doorframe to steady herself. Marian's shrieks stabbed into her ears.

Jaden's knees buckled. Bobbi kept her from slumping to the floor.

Bill was trying to hold Marian still and pull her to an area away from the shattered glass of the display case and jumble of knives. Her thrashing had loosened the knife so that it fell on the floor. Bobbi watched as Bill retrieved it, closed the blade, and slipped it into one of the glass shelves of a still intact display case. His dark eyes caught Bobbi's and she nodded silently in agreement with what he had done. *Tampered with evidence.* Protecting Jaden meant more to both of them.

Bobbi completely understood Marian's falling off the cliff of sanity. She might have done the same thing herself. Somehow a few good friends and her own determination helped her through the worst days of her life.

"I want to tell you what happened," Jaden began. "She killed Vincent after she realized that

279

he killed Sergio. There was no life for her without that sleazy man."

"Can you stop her screaming?" Bobbi asked.

"She's gone into another world," Bill cried over the wailing. "The medics will give her a shot to quiet her. She was going to kill you."

"And make it look like a robbery," Bobbi explained what she knew. "It was Vincent's idea."

"We should call her sister." Jaden could stand without trembling. She pressed down the bloody paper towels on her stinging arms, but she could only do one at a time.

Bill took Bobbi's place at her side. "How are you doing?"

"I'm...I'm. I don't know," Jaden confessed. "It was horrible. Marian hid in the bathroom. She pulled everyone away from here with made up stories. Bobbi saved me. What is this outfit? Disguise! Why didn't you tell me?"

Bobbi's dirty clothes were now stained with Jaden's blood.

"It's a long story. I was watching you and all of a sudden I couldn't help. I jabbed with the end of one of the patio umbrellas to break a window."

Bill was holding Jaden close and stroking her hair. "The medics are coming."

The siren drowned out Marian. Jaden nodded, suddenly unable to talk.

The emergency crew came, and, after an examination of Marian and an explanation from Bill, they gave Marian a shot. By the time they put her on the gurney, she was quieting.

"Can I help you, Ma'am?" the medic asked.

Bill took the paper towels off her arms. The glass cuts stung badly now and were covered with sticky blood, but had stopped bleeding.

"These are mostly superficial. I'm going to put on some medication and wrap your arms. Do you want to go to the hospital? Do you feel dizzy? What is your name?"

Jaden shook her head. "No. No. I'm Jaden Steele. This is, or was, my store. How am I ever going to clean this?"

"Robbery gone wrong, huh? I know this is going to sting. It will stop in a minute and you will feel much better."

He was right. Tears sprang to her eyes.

Bill told the medic, "Witnesses said the woman on the gurney fired her gun. Hit the display case and glass flew everywhere."

"Good thing she had bad aim. She'll be zonked out until tomorrow noon."

"When she fired, I ducked toward the door trying to get out."

"You're lucky." The man finished his gauze wrap with tape. "This place is a glass house. She must have been looney to fire a gun in here."

"She was crazy. She kept rambling and ordered me to open the safe. That lady over there saw what was happening and tried to distract her."

"Must have been just enough to make her shot miss," the medic said. "Lucky."

"Lucky," Bobbi echoed.

"Do you have a home, ma'am?" the medic asked, obviously eyeing her clothes.

"Yes," Bobbi snapped. "Right upstairs in apartment number two."

The EMT's eyebrows went up and he asked Jaden, "Can you sign this form? You are going to consult your own physician."

By the time the emergency crew left with Marian, she was asleep.

"I live right upstairs in apartment number one. I'd just like to go up to sleep."

"I'll vouch for these two," Bill said.

"Will you be handling the investigation?"

"Yes, I will."

"Let's get her upstairs," Bobbi said.

Bill held Jaden's shoulders with one strong arm. "The shop!" she protested.

"I'll call the security service. You are going to bed."

"I won't sleep. I never threw at a living person before. Her screams still ring in my ears."

"You saved your life. Sometimes you have to do things that you hate, Jaden. We'll be working all night here. The team won't be finished until dawn because of the work needed in the gallery. Bobbi, will you stay with her?"

"Of course I will," Bobbi answered from behind them.

Bill nodded. At Jaden's door he reluctantly took his arm away from her. He felt a tidal wave of relief sweep over him as Bobbi helped her with the door key. Tonight he could have lost her. When he heard the gunshot, his heart never stopped thundering. Even now it was racing.

He drew his gun on the run, diving into the court. The thought of losing Jaden made him want to scream, almost like that pathetic wife of Sergio's. A scream trapped itself in his throat.

The dark haired woman with the blue-violet eyes meant more to him than he realized. Up to now, canvas and paint had been the object of his passions. His heart finally slowed. When he saw her alive, he wanted to take her in his arms and hold her until to the other side of forever. At the same time he knew she was not ready for any relationship. Some time in the future she would be, and he would be there. His fingers felt numb. All this time he had been clutching the gun in his right hand. He relaxed his stiff fingers, put the safety back on, and slipped it into the holster. When the team was able to get to the shop, he would go to Monterey Hospital to see if Vincent was able to talk. He would have to check on Marian's condition. After he gathered all the information and wrote a report, it might be next spring. He would have to talk to the District Attorney before he drowned in the sea of computer forms.

Bill felt the muscles in his neck and shoulders finally relax. Even if the efforts took until next year, they would be worth it, though, because now Jaden, Esther, Roberta Petra Jones Schmidt, and the others who might have been targets were safe. The nightmare in Dolores Court was over.

"Do you have any brandy, Jaden?" Bobbi asked, sighing deeply.

"There's a bottle that I've never opened in the cupboard above the refrigerator. But if I have some now, I will pass out."

"It's for me," Bobbi responded with a slight grin. "You can join me if you want. Anyway, if you go to sleep right away that would be the best thing for you. Remember I had to watch you and Marian and I was desperate to get into the shop. It was my fault too, for not noticing that Marian went into the store."

"You did enough. Thank you. Why didn't you tell me about the homeless get-up?" Jaden sank down to the sofa. "I didn't recognize you until you spoke in the store."

"Edward Stennis suggested playing the part. I knew that I was good at disguises. You know that for the last six months I've been playing at being another person."

"Stennis?" Jaden's dark blue eyes, rimmed with red, turned to stare at her. "Stennis, as in Esther Stennis? Old Uncle Edward? Something else no one told me? I knew something was wrong about his sudden appearance here."

"He came because of Esther, but he had investigated every one of us first."

Jaden murmured, "You were the old woman outside of Za'tar's."

Bobbi's insides warmed with the brandy. "We watched you and McKenzie."

Jaden groaned, "You watched us? Spying?"

"We did not mean to intrude, Jaden. We were trying to keep you safe. And you didn't tell me about Esther. Bill and Edward explained."

She poured two glasses of brandy and handed one to Jaden. "You need to change your clothes. Those are dotted with glass. Sorry but I'll throw them away."

"I understand. It's all right, Bobbi," she assured her in a quiet voice, trying to unbutton her blood-spattered blouse.

Her friend went into the bedroom and finally returned with her old blue sweatsuit.

"Jaden, you are so lucky. McKenzie obviously likes you. Bill does, too. He did not want to turn loose of you down there. And I apologize for not realizing your ability with the knife. You are an expert. They terrify me. Let me throw that blouse away. Put on the sweatpants."

She paused. Jaden slipped off her bloodied gray slacks and let them drop to the floor. Her eyes were half closed. Bobbi lifted the pants from the floor and put both clothing items in the garbage under the sink. She finished the final swallow of her own warming brandy, and took her and Jaden's glasses to the sink. Before she washed the glasses, she pulled Jaden's feet up onto the sofa and slipped off her shoes. She covered her with a very old log cabin quilt.

To her surprise Jaden was still awake and murmured, "Thank you, Bobbi. My eyes won't open. I think they are pasted shut. Everything is throbbing and stinging."

"Sleep is the best thing for you right now."

Jaden was asleep. Bobbi watched her delicate features finally relax.

Because Bobbi did not want to leave her friend alone tonight, she went into the extra bedroom and sank to Jaden's bed.

Like Jaden's, her own eyes closed immediately.

Jaden woke to a bright autumn sun streaming in the windows. The odor of coffee filled the apartment. Nightmares plagued her during her sleep but they dissolved in the bright morning. For a few seconds she felt disoriented. Where was her bed? Her eyes opened wide. She was on her sofa. Her arms stung. She saw that they were bandaged.

"Morning," Bobbi waved a steaming mug of coffee under her nose.

Jaden sat straight up. She fought the sudden dizziness. "Bobbi? It wasn't a nightmare."

At the same time that Bobbi said, "It all did

happen," there was a knock at the door.

She opened the door and Uncle Edward stepped in. He was carrying a white plastic bag with several take-out containers inside.

"How is Jaden this morning?"

He placed the three containers on the table. "You'd think that there would be one fast food restaurant in this town. There isn't."

"I could have told you that," Bobbi pulled silverware from a drawer.

"I got these from that restaurant a block away. Scrambled eggs, hash browns, and biscuits. Nothing like a plate of cholesterol to start the morning right."

"Jaden, this is Edward Stennis, Esther's son. He told me about his mother. The others are going to be mighty unhappy about the deception."

"I know. I've felt horrible lying."

"Bill was trying to protect her. How are you?" Edward peered at Jaden with narrowed, concerned sky blue eyes.

Jaden looked at him and recognized Esther's clear blue eyes. "My ears are ringing. I'm trying to organize everything that happened in my mind. Bobbi was in that get-up. She saved me by distracting Marian for a few seconds. I'm sure that she saved my life."

"The disguise was my idea. We were all trying to protect you, too. I'm sorry I wasn't there last night. I should have been here! As soon as I heard Bill's story, I tried to drive over from Monterey and got stuck on the freeway because of an accident."

"I'm lucky Bobbi was there, no matter what she was wearing."

"I was trying to break the glass in the top of the door with the end of one of those patio umbrellas," Bobbi explained. "Those display windows are tough."

"Vincent killed Sergio and Jonah. I finally realized that," Jaden explained. "When he told Marian, she shot him. He also told her we were very close to the truth. She wanted to kill me."

"She and Vincent figured out how to get rid of the people who were staying around you," Edward said. "The only thing Vincent did not plan was to get himself shot. Marian left a message for McKenzie to return to San Diego. She called about Sandy's mom's emergency. She reported the break-in at the art gallery to bring the police over there. She guessed that the force is so small that Bill would come over."

Jaden told them, "Vincent took away her whole world when he killed Sergio. He was continually unfaithful, stole money, and she was blind to all of that. Vincent did not understand."

"She wasn't blind to it," Bobbi said. "Trying to rationalize her husband's behavior probably pushed her over the edge. She blamed everyone else except for the guilty one, Sergio. She was living a fantasy. It happens a lot. I know because for years I thought my husband would stop abusing me if I did whatever he said. He just became worse. Jaden, come and eat something."

Jaden slowly stood up and Edward pulled out her chair.

"Thank you. Thank you for everything, even for being a bag lady, Bobbi."

They all laughed.

Another knock on the door silenced them.

Bill's tall frame filled the doorway. He looked pale and exhausted. His dark eyes fixed on Jaden and he moved to her. "How are you?" He took her hands gently and stared at her bandaged arms, shaking his head.

"My arms sting. I'm lucky, though."

"Would you like some breakfast? Coffee?" Bobbi asked, her golden eyes sparkling with tears.

"No thanks. I need to get to bed."

"You've been up all night." Jaden said.

"At least the murders are solved and you and Bobbi are safe now. We have Vincent's confession. The doctors tell us that he probably won't make it. It was too long after the shooting before he got treatment. He lost too much blood."

"And Marian?" Edward asked.

"Still sleeping. We may never be able to question her. I need to go to bed now. I'll see you all, probably tomorrow. It's going to take a long time to sort this out."

"Get a good night's sleep, Bill. You need it."

After he left Bobbi said, "Did you notice that for Bill the two of us were barely in the room?"

"Yes, I did." Edward answered with a smile.

Bobbi lifted a forkful of hash browns.

Jaden actually felt her face grow hot. She did not respond to their teasing. Her thoughts went to Bill's dark eyes filled with concern. What made her suddenly think about her husband, Brent, who was like a best friend? McKenzie was that same type of man. Sergio was all charm and romance. Bill, though, stirred something in her that almost frightened Jaden. She decided that the feelings, whatever they were, could be dangerous.

Jaden learned enough to ignore someone like Sergio. Men like Bill were too moody and unpredictable. Holding onto him might be like trying to stop the ocean waves from hitting the shore. *I'm the opposite of Bill. I'm a practical businesswoman. His works of art are compelling.*

After their return Kyle and Sydney gave an exclusive high tea in Dolores Street Court on a Friday afternoon when every seagull on the central coast became a tourist visitor to the court. The birds lined up on the apartment railing.

The chefs and Enrique bustled around making sandwiches and scones and setting up a buffet on one of the tables. All of the court residents were invited as well as the shop owners. Gene Miller and the others were deep in conversation about some sale.

Amanda Perkins, the library director, came

with Bobbi and several of the library employees. Edward escorted his mother, Esther.

Kyle gave her a big bear hug "My dear, you came back from the dead miraculously. And you look good, too."

"Thank you, Kyle. I'm delighted to have a decade of enjoying life ahead of me."

McKenzie was telling Jaden, "My offer on the condo has been accepted and it's in escrow."

"That's wonderful, McKenzie. Isn't that wonderful, Bobbi?" Kyle asked.

Bobbi nodded and grinned, "Wonderful." She wondered how Bill would take that news. And they say small towns are dull.

"I'm looking for property, too," Esther's son told them. "This is a beautiful area. I can see why those Bohemian artists and writers like Jack London, and Mary Austin, and Robinson Jeffers came here at the beginning of the twentieth century. It's haunting."

His last two words surprised Jaden because she felt the same way. And she was surrounded by a group of friends who made her feel comfortable. The scars on her arms were superficial and, though some might be permanent, she felt lucky considering that the gunshot must have barely missed her. She believed in her grandma's words that she must have been spared for some reason.

Hal and Sandy had come to tea as well.

Ron walked into the court and said hello to everyone. "You'll join us, Ron?" Sydney brought over more chairs. "We're going to have a toast."

"I'm off duty," Ron said with a smile. "My good luck. Bill should be here soon."

Sydney started back for the café door, "We have the best coffee in town if he is still on duty."

"Now my friends," Kyle began. "Although this is high tea, we have brought out some champagne for this occasion. Everyone take a glass. Enrique has poured them all, and Enrique, you will join us. I would like to toast Esther, and we are so thrilled to have you back among the living. We understand the deception. To Jaden, and Bobbi, and their new lives with us."

Edward Stennis stood up, "To Mom, Jaden, and Bobbi. Congratulations to three beautiful, observant women."

Jaden relaxed with each sip of champagne. It never took many of the fine bubbles to relax her.

She looked over at McKenzie, who was saying, "Vincent confessed everything before he died. Marian is not much better mentally. In fact, she may never stand trial for anything. If she stays in that condition, the court will probably send her directly to an institution."

"But she killed Vincent," Bobbi protested. "And planned to kill Jaden. She deliberately made those phone calls to draw Hal and McKenzie and Bill away. That's premeditation."

"Under grave duress. Certainly there's no doubt she killed Vincent."

"It's over, anyway," Jaden said, relaxing even more. Her eyes wanted to close.

They were interrupted by a loud, "Meow."

"Where is that cat?" Bobbi asked.

Kyle opened the door of a cat carrier under one of the empty tables in the court. He drew out a long haired white cat with a spotted face and a fluffy whitetail. Jaden heard the animal purr from ten feet away.

"This is Arizona," Kyle introduced the cat to each one of them. "We heard him for about a day and a half and finally found him behind some sagebrush, meowing."

Sydney said, "We tacked notices everywhere and gave flyers to vehicles as they came through. No one claimed him and the animal shelter was full. They said there was little chance for some of the animals and they would be put to sleep."

Jaden stared into the amber eyes of the cat. She was startled because they reminded her of Bobbi's eyes. The animal seemed to be looking right into her mind. "Look at those eyes. No wonder the Egyptians worshipped them."

Kyle walked to Esther. "We're giving him to you for your 'rebirth,' Esther, as a tribute to a great lady. Now we can give him to you to enjoy."

The white fluff jumped right into her lap.

Esther beamed.

Arizona purred.

It crossed Jaden's mind that they were all outcasts from their own storms.

"I'm certain his majesty has found the best possible home."

Bobbi added, "Just like the rest of us."

Hal added, "I don't think this court is ever going to be the same."

Jaden felt more than a little tipsy after her second glass of champagne and knew it was time for her to go upstairs. "I'm not much of a drinker. I'll go to bed early tonight." She knew she would go right to sleep.

"I'll help you upstairs," McKenzie stood up.

"Good evening, Jaden," Hal said. "See you in the morning. Get some rest."

"Thank you, McKenzie," Jaden said as they were going up the stairs. "I should never have more than one glass of champagne."

"Your face is pink," He answered with a smile. "Look, there's something on your door. Wonder how it got up here."

It was a small package, actually a small brown paper bag, tied with string. A loop of string held it on the doorknob.

Jaden lifted the package from the knob and peered inside. There was a small, square object in a plastic bag. She pulled out a frame.

"It's a miniature painting," McKenzie said.

Jaden let the paper bag drop to the ground and held up the picture.

She held the frame and blinked. "It's lovely." The canvas itself was small, no more than six by eight inches. Waves rolled onto a beach. Jaden could almost feel the soft white sand. "It's beautiful." She squinted to read the small letters that spelled Aram.

"It's a wonderful painting," McKenzie spoke with envy. "Bill did it."

She went over to the wrought iron railing to look down on the group gathered in the court. "He's not here yet or I would go thank him."

"Ron said that he has been conferring with the District Attorney in Salinas."

"I'll have to thank him later," Jaden said, clutching the picture, not quite believing that he had painted this especially for her.

"It's actually a valuable painting," McKenzie told her.

Jaden knew the effort it must have taken to paint it.

"McKenzie, I am worried about Marian. Do you think she will be in an institution for a long time? A good long time?"

"No telling," McKenzie answered. "I know what I would ask as her attorney. All the circumstances involved might lead a judge to be lenient with her."

Jaden groaned to herself.

"Thank you for helping me up to the apartment, McKenzie. I am really tired."

"My pleasure, Jaden." He kissed her softly on her forehead. His kiss felt comforting.

She entered her apartment with the painting held tightly to her. McKenzie turned to walk down the stairs wondering if he could ever compete with the soft white sand in that tiny painting of the beach and the ocean. He had never seen Jaden that happy.

He joined the group at the tables in the court and downed two more glasses of champagne himself. McKenzie knew he was not going to be the same again, so he knew Hal was right about Dolores Street Court.

Difficult to believe that evil in the form of murder took place here. Because of his work, McKenzie knew that evil lurked everywhere, even in the most beautiful settings. He looked around the bright, white flagstone court with its planter boxes of yellow snapdragons and violet pansies. No wonder tourists and locals came to sit at these tables and have a drink or a sandwich from The Mad Hatter's. He was glad his offer on the condo in Monterey had been accepted. And, to be honest with himself, two of the most intriguing women he had ever met, Petra and Jaden lived here.

The shadow of a man fell across the table.

"Bill!" Esther said. "Sit down. Join us!"

"Who is that in your lap, Esther?" Bill sat down next to her, but he was looking around the table for Jaden, McKenzie thought.

Esther lifted up the cat, who was so relaxed that he looked like a white fur shawl.

"I think he could be a guard cat," Bill said with a slight smile. "Is Jaden upstairs?"

"She was tired," McKenzie told him. "She loved the painting that you gave her."

Bill's dark eyes stared intently at McKenzie. "Thank you," he said with a smile.

"She is still worried about Marian," Bobbi told him. "In her condition, will she be charged? The woman is dangerous."

Bill sank back in the chair. "The truth is that she probably never will be. Abby has arranged for her to go to an institution in northern California.

Depending upon what the courts and the doctors say, they may keep her there indefinitely for her own protection and everyone else's."

The group at the table groaned in a chorus.

McKenzie and Bobbi looked at each other and then at Bill, who was shaking his head. "The D.A. has Vincent's confession. For all anyone knows, Marian lost her mind when Vincent told her that he had killed Sergio. She killed him in an insane rage."

Bobbi looked around the table. "Doesn't that worry anyone else? She could be released. Marian planned to murder Jaden. Sergio's murder stole her whole world."

McKenzie answered, "You know that Lady Justice is blind. Marian may use an insanity defense. There should be a way to plead guilty but insane. Temporary insanity covers too much."

Bobbi frowned. A wave of outrage swept over her. Would she ever recover from the hurt and misery of her own trial? Marian, who was guilty, might never have to spend a day in court.

Hal spoke up. "It's over, anyway. Now our two amateur women detectives can retire and return to their regular jobs."

"Kyle, let's have one more toast. To a return to a normal, quiet life in Dolores Street Court."

Lifting his water glass, Kyle answered,

"Like Hal, I strongly suspect that Dolores Court will never be the same again."

Jaden sat on the sand of Asilomar beach, watching the swirling, frothing surges crash against the jagged granite rocks of the point. She had tried for several weeks to decide whether she should stay in the central coast.

Finally she made her choice. The waves called to her like the sirens in legend called to ships. Whether she crashed or whether she found her way to port, this bay felt like home.

Jaden was so lost in the compelling sea that it took a few seconds for her to realize that someone cast a shadow behind and over her. As the waves foamed and churned on the etched deep brown rocks of the point, she turned to face the shadow.

About the Author

Barbara Chamberlain was awarded First Place for her fantasy novel, *The Flight of Alpha I*, at the 2011 Arkansas Writers Conference. In 2009 her original Okinanawan fable, "A Bowl of Rice," won the Writers Digest Contest for juvenile/young adults.

Her award winning books, *The Prisoner's Sword* and *Ride the West Wind* were named Recommended Reading by the National Council of Teachers of English.

She received a Masters in Library and Information Science at San Jose State University. Her bachelor's degree in history is from UC Santa Cruz.

Barbara was a librarian at Monterey City Library and Harrison Memorial Library in Carmel. There she began to write *A Slice of Carmel*. She conceived the novel's characters on walks through Carmel village.

Look for the sequel, *Slash and Turn*. The visit of a well-known touring Russian ballet company to the Monterey Bay turns deadly. Jaden Steele, Bobbi Jones, and the residents of Dolores Court travel through a maze of dance company members and tragic history to unravel the puzzle of murder.

Currently, Barbara is the Northern California President of The National League of American Pen Women. She enjoys storytelling, leading creative writing and storytelling seminars and is a member of The National Storytelling Network and the Cabrillo Host Lions Club.

Made in the USA
Charleston, SC
26 November 2011